The Scarring

of the

Roshanra

The Scarring

of the

Roshanra

Kara SB Brown

This book is dedicated to my father, Ernest J. Stevens, who served in the Vietnam War and passed away from side effects when he was fifty-seven, while I was away on active duty. I miss you always, Daddy.

A second dedication is to my love, Kenyon, who has helped me learn to be more independent and confident in myself. And for accepting who I am, weirdness and all.

Finally, to our emotional support dog, Lana, who passed away 1 Feb 2021, after four years in chemotherapy. We miss you, sweet pup!

Kara Stevens, writing under the pen name Kara SB Brown, is a disabled veteran with PTSD and other comorbid issues. She lives in her head more than reality and writes dark psychological fantasies as a cathartic exploration into her traumas, including therapy skills she's learned over the years. When not writing, Kara sings, dances around without style, practices Muay Thai and yoga, meditates, paints, draws, learns instruments or languages, helps train her fiancé's and her own service dogs (she even dances with them!), enjoys time with their two cats, and loves to be with her fiancé, who she met in Afghanistan.

THE SCARRING OF THE ROSHANRA

SIGN UP FOR THE MONTHLY NEWSLETTER

To receive special offers, giveaways, discounts, bonus content, updates from the author, info on new releases, emotional healing tips, and much more:

https://earnestsbbrown.com

KARA SB BROWN

1

Kala sat on her shower floor underneath a stream of hot water, as hot as she could get it. She held her knees to her chest and rocked back and forth, watching from behind a protective screen in her mind which she had had her whole twenty-four-year-life. Blood swirled down the shower drain. Water diluted the thick red liquid to a thin, pink stream. She dug her fingers into her knees to push back unwanted memories and compared the small chunks of congealed blood with stones pushed downstream. Tears fell, indistinguishable from the hot stream of water. This time, the blood was not only hers. *This can't be real ... please, don't let this be real!*

Her legs shook as she stood. She held the grab bar as vertigo hit, wobbled, then caught her balance. Her ears rang just before her mind reconnected with her body. She needed to see. She needed to know. The lack of clarity sent thorns deep into her mind and she felt the bile rising. She swallowed and gritted her teeth. Her face throbbed and inflammation burned as she ignored the pains. Had she imagined the fiery fist? How had she broken the glass in which to stab him? How had the shards come into her hand? Too many questions, not enough answers. She focused back on the present.

Blood and water dripped from her hair onto her shoulders. Her nerves spiked, as if they clattered up a spiral staircase, running into the rails on each side as they panicked with her mind. She aimed shampoo into her hand and hissed when it poured down the drain. With a screech of agony, she swiped her non-injured hand to collect any shampoo that had not breached the drain. She did not care that blood had mixed with the shampoo. She would never get it all off, anyway. She took a deep breath, hissing again as a stabbing pain shot through her ribs.

After vigorously cleaning the rest of her body, she stepped out and dried off, avoiding the mirror. It would only show her what she knew to be true; she was broken, inside and out.

It was times like this when she yearned for her twin flame, for the hugs he could provide, for the care he offered her when she needed it. She yearned to call Daniel. She used her non-dominant hand to pick up the phone, only then seeing the bandage on her hand. When did she wrap it? Had she blacked out again?

She put the phone back down. No. He'd broken up with her, had his own problems. He didn't need more of hers. It was why they weren't together anymore... But she didn't know what else to do.

I have to do something. I'll call the police. It's the right thing to do. Maybe it will be okay...

"Nine-one-one. What's your emergency?"

Kala looked over at the dead man again. Fear and self-loathing burned within her; she trembled and cried.

The detectives walked her out. "We need to get you to the hospital first. Medical exam. Do you consent?"

Kala nodded, feeling apprehensive about the exam. "I'm sorry I showered," she said, talking faster than normal. "It was impulsive—I had so much blood on me. But he didn't rape me... I didn't... let him..." Sobs went in and out as her brain disconnected and reconnected with reality.

"We'll go over everything with the medical examiner. Shhh... it's over. You're okay."

Kala's crying intensified. The detectives looked concerned. *They know I'm crazy. They see it.* They would blame her. He was dead and she was alive—no one would believe she was strong enough; they'd think she'd planned it.

"Stop!"

The detectives halted, alarmed. "What's wrong?" Detective Campbell turned around. "Did we miss something?"

"No," Kala said, head bowed in shame. "My brain. I'm sick of it. I just want it to stop..."

"I understand. We can set you up with a therapist. You've been through an ordeal."

Kala shook her head. She had seen therapists for years. Been through what seemed like dozens of therapies. "It... doesn't help. Nothing will help."

They arrived at the hospital in less than fifteen minutes. Detective Campbell took Kala into the emergency entrance and talked with the nurses. A short wait later, Kala was on an examination table, nausea rolling her stomach until she felt she might faint.

The medical examiner assessed the damage and took the detectives across the room, whispering to them and showing them her chart. Her heightened senses allowed her to hear his whispers and she could feel his energy. He sounded clinical, but his energy seemed... cautious and sympathetic. She had several broken ribs, a busted lip, black eye, spiral fractures in her left wrist, a quarter-inch gash in her right palm, and a sprained ankle. The only area left undamaged seemed to be her genitals.

She looked down at her hand which now itched from the stitches. She couldn't tell anyone what really happened. They would never believe her, and she would be hospitalized, put on medications that just made her worse.

The medical examiner confirmed she had been attacked. The coroner would autopsy the man, figure out how he died. They could compare notes with what Kala told them.

When they had arrived at the Murfreesboro, Tennessee police station, Detective Campbell put her in an interrogation room, remodeled for victims to answer questions. In place of the hard folding chairs one would see on TV and in small-town police departments, an armchair sat opposite the interviewer. It reminded Kala of a therapist's office. It was better than she had expected.

"Do you need anything? Coffee? Water?"

"Water. Thank you." Kala's voice sounded distant again. The jitters had left her, and all she felt was exhaustion... and sadness... and sickness.

She looked at the clock on the wall. It was almost five o'clock. If her calculations were correct, the attack had happened during the witching hour. *That figured…* most violent crimes against her had happened around this time. Kala heard long ago that supernatural entities preferred three to four o'clock as their "playtime". It was also known as the Devil's Hour. *Did the Devil come for me again?*

Detectives Campbell and Shadow came into the room. Detective Shadow held a clipboard and pen—the hideous smirk on his face when seeing Kala's nervousness made him look punchable, and his vile energy stuck to her like slime. Kala smoothed her face, hiding the sneer that threatened to show itself. Detective Campbell held a glass and a pitcher of water. She placed them on the table next to Kala.

"We found your wallet," Detective Shadow spoke. "You're a veteran?"

Kala nodded.

"What branch were you?"

"Air Force." Her voice was quiet. "Linguist," she added.

"Oh, I was too. Military Police. Made sense to join the police force."

Kala could tell he was trying to bond with her. Her stomach churned.

Detective Shadow switched tactics. "We called the VA. They're contacting your next of kin. We also see you have a permanent and total service-connected disability. Do you want to talk about it?"

Kala shook her head. "No."

Detective Campbell took over. "Please, tell us what happened. Whatever you can remember would help."

"It's foggy. I'll do my best." She closed her eyes and took a deep breath. "I was prepping for bed again—nightmares kept me awake." Nightmares that seemed real. Where her father lived a half-life and warned her of the danger she faced. "I had dried off and was brushing my teeth. Still... not dressed. I heard a noise outside my room..." She had felt his noxious presence before she heard any noise. "I'm not sure how." She looked imploringly to each of the officers. They had to believe her, she hoped they believed her.

She took a sip of water. "I donned my robe and opened my bedroom door." Kala's body tensed and she felt every injury she had ignored before. She winced but continued her story. "That's when he... hit me." She looked at the cops. "I'd never been punched in the face before, at least not by a human."

When Detective Campbell raised her eyebrow, Kala chuckled, a habit she'd had all her life when she needed to calm down.

She took a deep, painful breath. "Sorry, that was unclear. My ex-husband threw a TV remote at my lip once. He liked to see me cry. A horse that I helped train panicked when my brother rode a go-cart by and threw its head down on mine when I was fifteen, and I've fallen on my face a few times in my life." Her mind raced and she sighed, resisting the urge to massage the tension points around her wounds. "I never thought it would hurt this bad."

An urge to clarify more tugged at her mind, but she repressed it. Her body remembered the abuse from her marriage yet her mind had been abused even more. Images floated through her mind: scenes from the past, all the abuses she endured by a husband who considered himself a pimp. Elbows to the ribs or stomach, thrown to the ground from his shoulders, forced to sleep with his friends then blamed for it, but nothing compared to the pain now spiking through her body, like a compilation of every injury she had ever endured.

Her eye swelled more each minute. She had rejected a cold pack earlier, stating it brought on migraine pains. Regret for declining its icy assistance rushed to the surface.

Detective Campbell pulled her chair closer to Kala and spoke in a softer tone, as if she could sense Kala's pain levels rising. "Did you know the man?"

"I'm not sure. I think he worked for the apartment complex. A creepy guy. If it's the same one, I reported him. They said he was 'harmless', schizophrenic." Kala shook her head. "It's not always harmless…" She paused again. She began to shiver, despite the warm clothing.

"What happened next? Please continue."

"I fell to the floor. He kicked me. A lot. Then he undid his belt and jeans button. Before he could undress, I kicked back, wild and as hard as I could. I couldn't see, just felt him. Tripped him… He fell, landing on top of my legs. My ankle twisted under him. I felt… like he was crushing me." Kala's brow was creased while she spoke, trying to recall as much as possible; yet not knowing what was real or what was perceived. She knew she had bruises and cuts to prove her story but always doubted her memory.

"I found some broken glass next to me… I think I knocked it off the table. I grabbed it… stabbed at him until he stopped moving. I think I got his neck and face. Maybe stomach. It's all a blur… I just… I didn't want it to happen again. Never again."

Kala bent over crying, snot smearing her freshly bandaged hands. Her body clenched so tight, she felt she would never relax.

The words he said, words she would not share, echoed in her mind. *You belong to the goddess of shame; she will have your soul.*

Detective Campbell refilled Kala's water glass before questioning further. "What do you mean, never again? Had he done something before?"

Kala lost control of her mind. She attempted to breathe and hyperventilated instead. The pressure increased in her head; stabbing pains shot through her right eye. Migraine on top of the night she'd had. "Ice… please?" Those were the only two words which would make it through for another twenty minutes.

When they brought the ice pack, Kala put it on the back of her neck. She second-guessed herself then put the ice on her eye. A sharper pain jolted through her right eye, the same one in which the fiery fist landed.

When she could breathe again, Detective Campbell said, "There's someone on the phone for you. Can you take a call?"

"Okay," she sniffed, still stuffy from crying. The detectives left her alone.

"Kala? Are you there?" A deep, soothing voice called out to her from the other end of the phone line. How could he know? She must be imagining things; she had wanted so bad to talk to Daniel. Had her mind manifested this call? She stood and paced, energy surging through her. The phone hurt her face and she had trouble holding it, so she switched to the speaker phone and sat back down, tapping her feet to the tune of the lullaby he created for her.

"Kala?"

"Daniel?" She sobbed through a small smile. "Is that you?"

"Yeah. Are you okay?" She could hear the love in his voice, the love that could soothe all her aches. She leaned closer to the phone,

11

envisioning his handsome face with the high cheekbones and wolf-like grin.

"I ... will be. How did you know?"

"The VA called me. I'm still your emergency contact... Sorry I can't be there."

"No, don't be. I'm not your responsibility. I didn't want to bother you... How are you?"

Daniel laughed, but it was halfhearted. "You're at the police station and you're asking me how I am?"

Kala let out a dry laugh. "Yeah, you're right. I want to go home... I don't mean where I've been living. I mean... I miss you."

"I know, sweetie. You must stay there right now. I called your mom. Marnie said you can stay with her. I'm not ready yet."

"I know. I'm... sorry." *I always do this. I always say the wrong thing.* "I'm not trying to force you..."

"Don't be sorry," he interrupted. "Stop beating yourself up. You've had a hard night. I love you. Get some rest."

"I love you, too." The line disconnected. "Bye..." Sadness enveloped Kala; it had been a hopeless belief that her life would improve.

The detectives finished their questioning but her mind closed off, wouldn't allow any answer to surface. She was shattered.

Detective Campbell led Marnie into the room an hour later, Detective Shadow no longer in tow. "Kala, your mother said you can stay with her as long as you need. We talked with the VA. They said you've shown progress in therapy but you're still high-risk. They will work with the patient advocates to get you out of your apartment lease. You don't need to be alone right now."

Kala agreed. She needed to be around people who loved her and cared about her. But she also needed quiet. Something she rarely got at Marnie's house. Still, she agreed to leave with her mother.

"We will need to interview you again later this week. May we come to your home? You don't need to drive here."

"Yes, that's fine."

As Marnie led Kala to her vehicle, she put an arm around her and pulled her in close. "I can see your pain; you don't have to bear this cross alone. I'm proud of you, Kalabear."

The drive to her hometown took an hour and a half. The mini-van's bucket seats were worn and uncomfortable. Kala fidgeted, unable to find relief. An order for pain killers was in the works but the pharmacy wasn't open yet, so she was forced to wait.

She didn't want to take medications; she always dissociated more when she had them, but she dissociated with pain too. Where was an end to the cycle? She was born with a lack of clarity, and the traumas in her life caused a greater disconnect from reality.

Kala could not comprehend anything Marnie said. Though she tried to listen, the communication seemed garbled, much like Charlie Brown's teacher in the *Peanuts* show. "Mah, mah, mah…"

"Momma, I'm sorry. I need quiet. My head hurts… a lot." Her mother turned the Christian music down. She still asked questions, which Kala answered in short sentences. Kala knew the urge to talk well, and couldn't fault Marnie, until she became so overwhelmed she plugged up her ears and pulled her sweatshirt hood down.

The sun peaked out over the horizon and Kala stared, mesmerized by the oranges, pinks, purples, and blues dancing around in her vision. Puffy white-grey clouds threatened rain, but rain wouldn't come today; even the clouds teased Kala.

As they left the Murfreesboro city streets, farms popped into view. Cows and horses grazed in pastures surrounded by trees and hills. She remembered this route well, had memorized the trees lining the roads, areas of shadow which relaxed Kala's mind. She loved the trees, the hills, the animals. Why couldn't life always be this peaceful? But wouldn't a peaceful life be boring as well? Something told her she had more to offer than she believed, but she pushed down that line of thought, just like she pushed down the negative thoughts.

They pulled into the hidden driveway to Marnie's house, Kala's childhood home. The gravel path made for a bumpy ride. She missed riding horses down this path and through the trees surrounding their house which was built into the hill.

Her younger brother, George, walked out as she stepped out of the car. He was twenty, almost three years younger than Kala, but towered over her. *Would I have been targeted as much if I was taller than five-foot-six?*

The brick house seemed familiar yet unfamiliar. Not much had changed, except the energies around her. A shadow of her father's energy remained three years after his death. She felt even lonelier than when she was alone.

The air seemed cold despite the summer heat. She focused her attention on the earth, as she was apt to do when she needed to ground her mind. Dew droplets sat on blades of grass, shaking as though they feared the sun. Clover speckled the ground. Finding four-leaf clovers had been a habit, one she enjoyed. If she found the right one, her heart's desires would come true. It had happened before, just before she deployed and met Daniel. It would happen again, if this wasn't a delusion of hers.

"Hey, Kala." George grabbed her and gave her a rough hug, a mischievous twinkle in his eyes. "You look rough, but you've always been clumsy. You should be used to the bruises."

"Ow." She smiled, despite the pain. "Good to see you, bud." She looked up at his face. The morning sun highlighted the greenish hue in his sky blue eyes.

"You, too. Sorry to hear what happened." Concern etched his face. He was reading her, figuring out what he could do to help. He was the reserved type, leaving her to her own devices unless she requested help. Like her father. Her family seemed to be composed of struggling empaths.

"Eh, it's life." Kala shrugged, reducing muscle tension in the process. "I seem to be a target." Kala believed that. She had been raped multiple times; other times, men had taken advantage of her apparent vulnerabilities, leading her to their emotional torture dens like cattle. She was paranoid, stupid. Crazy.

"Nah, you're just too nice."

Kala couldn't believe George called her nice. She had just killed a man! "Nice? Didn't Momma tell you what I did?"

"You're still nice." George smiled at her. "Here, let me get your bag."

"My bag?" She was confused.

"I told you, Kala," Marnie chimed in. "I stopped at your apartment before going to the police station. I got some clothes. You need more. There was nothing but gym clothes in your apartment. You need to dress more lady-like."

"Yeah, like dressing lady-like will get me *less* attention. Momma, the way I dress is unrelated. I need to rest." With a hug to her mother, and thanks to her brother, she walked down the porch and picked up a small black kitten. "She's going inside with me, okay?" She looked at her mother's face which showed both sorrow and irritability. Kala's mood swings always had this effect on her. "I'll clean up after her. I just need a furry friend right now."

"Okay, Kala," Marnie said with a grin. "It's not the first time you've convinced me to keep the pets indoors."

Kala walked inside, holding the door open for her brother and mother.

2

Kala spent the next four days resting as much as possible. Insomnia had taken its hold; fatigue caused more willfulness. The cute kitten, who she named Ninja Tulip, played on the bed next to her as she read her old books: *Goodnight Moon*, *Happy Birthday Moon*, *The Day Jimmy's Pet Boa Ate the Wash*. A part of her wished for the peace of those times but she was wiser now and wouldn't trade her knowledge, what little she had, for the world.

The police were done with the crime scene. She needed to get items from her apartment. Her medium-firm memory foam mattress was especially missed; fibromyalgia pain increased with her distress. Her muscles felt like fragments of brick. Her mind raced every day; she tried to figure out the situation, but her attacker's words hadn't made sense. Who was the goddess of shame? Was it symbolic, like he intended to cause her shame?

Either way, he had hurt her. Her life had been in danger. She didn't murder him. She had protected herself the only way she knew how. Yet depression enveloped her. She recalled the way it felt when he kicked her ribs. Looking back, she couldn't believe she hadn't felt the pain that morning. In the aftermath, breathing had become difficult, pain with each inhale and exhale. That was to be expected; it wasn't the first time the wind had been knocked out of her.

The thing that surprised her was how quickly she had grabbed the glass and plunged it into the man. His skin's resistance to being pierced had not deterred her. The glass was sharp enough; it slit open her own hand until she changed her grip. Then it seemed she controlled the glass without using her hands, but that was ridiculous. In her panic, she could have had psychosis, but she heard his flesh, his screams of rage, his vows that she would never win. She must have stabbed the man at least twenty times, frantic to be free. Safe.

All things considered, she was safe. Her military service had provided some self-defense and combat skills training although she learned more growing up and through self-study. She and Daniel had practiced on occasion; Daniel's service-connected sciatica and Kala's fibromyalgia flare-ups kept her from practicing more.

She heard the doorbell ring, which was out of the ordinary. They were miles out of town. Who would even come here? The doorbell was broken. George must have fixed it. She decided that whoever it was, they had nothing to do with her. She had no desire to see anyone in this town. Distrust rankled her spirit. She sighed.

"Hi. Is Kala around?" The voice came through the thin walls. It was Daniel.

She shot off the bed which took up most of the room, opened the door, and ran out. The startled kitten hissed and ran out too. Excitement flowed through her. She had not seen her love, her twin flame, in a year. Blind to her pain, she tackled Daniel, wrapping her arms around him, and pretended to gnaw on him like a zombie. He grunted and laughed. Her ribs screamed but she ignored them and hugged him tighter. He was there!

He pushed her back into a loose hug as his lips rested upon her forehead. Sadness permeated his eyes and his face reddened. She had increased his worries, and she had wanted to stop them.

Tears trickled down his cheeks as he said, "I wanted to come. I could tell you needed me. I wish I had been there for you... I'm sorry."

Kala wiped her tears on her bandaged hand. She studied his face, memorized the energy she felt from him; it was pure sadness with a hesitant love. His eyes glistened with tears and he looked away.

Through her sobs, she said, "Sorry? Why? You're here now. I'm okay, safe. I'll live. The pain will pass; even if it comes back, it will pass."

He sniffled and pulled a tissue pack from his pocket then offered her one. "Wow, you've come a long way..." He looked pleased and some of the redness left his face. "How are you so positive right now?"

She shrugged. "All things considered, this is not the worst thing that could have happened. I defended myself, even when I felt like I couldn't. That's improvement." She saw her reflection in the mirror. The bruised eye showed signs of healing, a yellow tinge beginning to form within the dark purple. Strange, her wounds seemed to heal faster these days. Still, her bright sky-blue eye appeared bloodshot in the small slit.

She wanted to laugh and cry at the same time. Daniel had traveled fifteen hours to see her, all the way from Minnesota, to comfort her. He still loved her. Maybe she could move back in with him and be around for the first snow.

No, she couldn't get her hopes up. Mental disorders were hard enough on their own without adding more confusion. He had said he wasn't ready to be back in a relationship with her. Couldn't he see how torturous this was to her sanity? Just as she saw his sanity suffered.

"Thank you for coming. You didn't have to, though…"

"Stop it, Kala." He was using his stern voice and face, the one that said, *I'm not kidding. Don't you dare cross that line!*

Her voice shook with laughter. "Do you want to go with me to get my things? I haven't gone yet; I just got the call that the police were done this morning."

"Sure. It's a good thing I brought my truck."

As they walked out, his warm hand rested on the small of her back. She gazed at him, studying his freckles and glowing cheeks. She wanted to memorize every freckle, maybe even name them. Pleasure filled her soul and she felt she would burst. Despite everything, he still loved her.

Daniel driving down the bumpy gravel driveway reminded Kala of when they first met in Afghanistan, working as contractors. She had been promiscuous, as she had been groomed to be, and had hated herself every time she gave in to that pressure to please people she despised. History repeated itself until she felt dead inside. Insanity.

She had never felt satisfaction until she met Daniel. There was a bond there, one she had not felt with any man other than her close family. They were friends, best friends, before they began dating. Over time, they learned how similar they were. Too similar, in fact. They both had PTSD, Borderline Personality Disorder, dissociative disorders, and intractable pain. Life was miserable, even on good days.

They would lose all sense of identity and perception, analyzing everything until all was evil in their lives—they were evil. Fear of abandonment and treachery filled their heads until they couldn't take any more. The constant anxiety and depression caused their relationship to become so turbulent they believed they could never be right for one another. Social media sites confirmed their thoughts. What they perceived to be manipulation by one another was a fear-based decision to show how they felt, no matter how intense the emotion was.

It seemed they had both decided to do what they felt was right, not what others manipulated them into doing. Kala wanted to talk about it but did not know what to say. She would start to say something, then stop. *He'll just think I'm a nag, or insensitive. I don't even know where to start! I'm so confused. I wish he would tell me what he's thinking.*

They drove the hour and a half, listening to music the entire way. Trees lined the highways in some areas, forming a tunnel which enticed Kala to breathe a sigh of relief. She loved nature. Daniel was the same.

"I'm feeling nervous about going back. I need a distraction. Can we talk?" Kala shivered, but not from cold. It had become a hot, humid day.

"Yeah. Anything in particular?"

"Well, what have you been up to lately?" She wanted to know but was scared to know.

"Mostly being alone. DBT and other VA appointments. Sometimes I would go to a friend's house, but that got old. I played some guitar and video games. Not much else."

Kala wanted to share her story, be as honest as possible. "I isolated a lot, but confusion led me to doing... things that make me cringe. I kind of blame myself for getting into the mess I had this week. I felt numb and mistook the physical feelings of anxiety for arousal. Impulsively messaged people for sex when I was really disoriented. When I would 'wake up' from dissociative episodes, which is what I call it because I feel like it's a dream, I would find messages that brought suicidal thoughts to my mind. I traced my veins as if I could find the answers to my questions inside. I went into the hospital for a while." She breathed in, noticing her pains had dampened after admitting her faults.

"After I left the hospital, I knew what I needed to do. Isolate, spend more time healing. That's when I noticed the creeper. His putrid energy stuck to me like the smell of the poo pond in Kandahar."

"When did all this start?" Daniel asked. His clenched jaw twitched, and his knuckles were white as he gripped the steering wheel.

Kala could feel his sadness and hatred, but who was the hatred directed toward? A deep shame resurfaced, but she pushed it back, refusing to be a pawn for some make-believe goddess. "I'm not really sure. It only lasted a couple of months. I decided I had had enough, recognized I wasn't that person, about a week before that… douchebag… broke in. I could have the timeline wrong. My brain still swims with images and emotions I can't put together. I'm so tired…"

"I understand. I'll be here tonight. I won't go anywhere." He said the words yet she sensed a new wall form inside him.

Still, a tentative warm sensation rose, one she had not felt in a long time. Hope. It was pulsing through her, giving back the life she once had, long ago when she was young. The feeling did not reach its threshold, but time would heal the rift between them.

They packed up her items as fast as they could. The bed was hardest; Kala tried to help but Daniel insisted that she rest her ribs.

Instead, her head swiveled; hyper-vigilance took over. She had the familiar sensation of being watched. She felt safer with Daniel there but still looked over her shoulder.

When they arrived back to her mom's house, George helped Daniel bring the bed inside. He had already removed the mattress from Kala's room, the room she slept in when she was a child. Kala and Daniel went to bed early that night shortly after they organized her items.

In Daniel's arms, she was free to dream. She walked through the woods in her mother's twenty-five acres. Leaves rustled in the wind. She closed her eyes, feeling her father's presence. It was warm, comforting, and appealing. Twigs crackled beneath her feet. Scents of earth and moss wafted through the air. She smelled the forest decay, knowing it would bring new life in the spring.

The scene turned dark. The sounds, from chirping birds to crackling twigs, stopped. When she gasped, no sound came out. She was alone. Scared. *If only I can light the path, I can get out. Purge the darkness from this place.*

She heard "This Little Light of Mine" echo within her mind. It was her voice, when she was a child. She thought of her father, James, then of Daniel as she heard his music in the wind, the lullaby he created as she slept next to him. The two people in the world she trusted most. James from her past, Daniel from her present and future. In a perfect world, they would all be together and form a bluegrass rock band.

Light shone from her hands. She looked down, amazed. Her palms were cool where she thought they would be warm. Breathing deeply, she outstretched her right palm. Something inside told her to visualize the forest lighting up. She closed her eyes, imagining the sun flickering through the treetops. Waves of light caressed her soul, which she felt move inside her.

She opened her eyes. The scene had changed again. Her body radiated light. The trees overhead lit up, illuminating the leaves' underside which would normally have been in shade. Daniel's and James' voices whispered in the wind, "Trust your instincts."

Kala woke refreshed, with less pain and sadness. She could move. She could breathe. Stretching, she leaned over and kissed Daniel on the cheek; he was still asleep. She stared at every freckle, memorizing the shapes they made. Here, a boat. There, a turtle. A constellation of freckles, which she had heard meant the ginger had stolen a soul. Whatever, he could have her soul. He would take care of it and give it back stronger than it was before.

She sneaked out of the bed and tucked him in then searched the kitchen. She found what she needed—bacon, eggs, flour, baking soda, salt, pepper, butter, milk, and lemon. Marnie seemed to be out of buttermilk. Kala would make biscuits, gravy, and bacon for everyone.

She sighed as she cracked the eggs and cooked bacon. Those poor little animals; their only role in life was to be eaten. Kala had tried vegetarianism, but she couldn't do it. Her body required less carbohydrates and more protein to function. If only she could create a delicious, magical protein source that did not kill or harm animals. What if she picked up fresh roadkill instead? That was a little better, right? No, more chances of disease. She squashed that idea as she kneaded the biscuit dough with her fingers.

Marnie came in while she was cooking. "Good morning, Kalabear."

Kala smiled and hugged her mother then chuckled. "Oops... you have flour in your hair now."

Marnie laughed with her as she put on a pot of coffee. "I'll make it stronger; I know that's how you and Daniel like it. I can just water it down with ice cubes."

Kala smiled.

"I'm going shopping today. Do you want to go with me? Meyers has some cute clothing, and I need more groceries." Marnie liked driving a little extra to get better quality and cheaper items; they were just over the border from Scottsville, Kentucky, where groceries ran untaxed. Bowling Green, Kentucky was another thirty or so minutes past Scottsville. Sometimes it seemed the extra mileage would negate that discount, but Kala knew better than to question her mother on things like this.

"I abhor shopping..." Decisions, people, public places, spending money? Ick. Others could have the habit. She just wanted to spend her money on pets, workouts, food, and other items for survival. Mental survival, too. "Did you fix the piano? I want to practice once my hands heal."

"No. I can have George look at it when the police leave; they called yesterday while you were out to say they would be by today. I have piano books you can borrow. The Bible, too."

Kala cringed. Since the first rape, she felt insecure when Christianity was mentioned. Divine intervention did not exist in her eyes. If it did, she must have deserved what she got. Why else would it have happened?

Marnie saw the look on her daughter's face; her own face fell. "I'll buy you some more art supplies. Do you want to draw or paint?"

Kala shrugged her shoulders. "I'm not sure I can do either well yet. At least paint supplies, maybe a sketch pad. I'll give you some money, if you don't mind getting them. I don't want to go anywhere..."

Kala could see both empathy and judgment in her mother's eyes. That was usually the case; she could tell her mother cared for her but thought she needed to do things the way she was taught, not learn her own strategies in life.

"Kala, you can't hide from the world."

"Yeah, but I can sure try." Bitterness showed through in her tone. An urge to snap came up; she let it pass. This was her mother, a woman who had cared for her for her entire life. She could never harm Marnie.

"I miss Daddy… I wish he was still here." The only time she had really felt a connection with anyone since his death was with Daniel.

"I know, Kala. His spirit is still here. God is with us, too."

Kala felt her subconscious scoff. "I'm going to take this food to Daniel." She didn't want to cry in front of her mother. She wanted to isolate. Be left to process her emotions.

Daniel ate with her as she thought about what had happened. The answers had to be somewhere, deep in her mind. If she sought them, they would come. She laughed at her thoughts and breathed in, closing her eyes. As she did, images of the fiery man rushing toward her flashed, mingling with other flashbacks from her life. So many shameful actions performed by her and against her. Then there was no thought. Her mind was blank.

Daniel called to her. Marnie was knocking on her door. "Kala, the police are here. Can you come out?"

"I'll be right there." Kala looked at Daniel, who stretched and stood.

"I'll go with you for support, but I will not interrupt the interview."

Kala smiled in appreciation and walked out into the living room. She sat on the couch across from another, where Detectives

Campbell and Shadow waited. With lemonade provided by Marnie. Ever the host, her mother.

"Did you sleep well?" Detective Campbell's sympathy showed.

"Not until last night," she said, pushing hard to think through the brain fog. "I felt safer with Daniel here."

"We have some more questions," Detective Shadow said with too much force. *He must be doing the good cop, bad cop routine.*

Detective Campbell glared at him; it must not have been approved beforehand. Kala wondered whether he did this with everyone or if he thought she deserved what she got.

"Why didn't you tell us you had Borderline Personality Disorder?" His tone was accusatory.

Daniel's fists clenched beside her and she placed her hand on his. With an almost imperceptible head shake, she answered. "It's a diagnosis. Not related to someone breaking into my home and attacking me." She heard the urgency in her voice, though she tried to stay calm.

"That may be true. Or, you could have lured him in there and attacked him."

Kala looked to Detective Campbell. Repulsion showed in her face, yet she said nothing. Kala could feel Daniel was rigid next to her. She breathed in and out, not looking away from Detective Shadow. She squashed the urge to grit her teeth and relaxed her tongue instead. "No. Why do you think that?"

"You're obviously crazy."

"That's enough, Detective Shadow!" Detective Campbell stepped in. "I'll ask the rest of the questions."

"I want to report him." Fury rose in Kala, affronted by his biased questioning. A fire flickered in her vision, stoked by the judgment in the detective's eyes. He didn't understand her at all—wasn't even trying to.

"Yes, you may. I'll give you the details before we leave."

Kala did not feel bad for asking in front of Detective Shadow. She was tired of douchebags getting their way. For the first time in her life, she felt she deserved respect. Daniel smiled at her, and she knew she had done the right thing.

The rest of the meeting went slower than molasses. Detective Campbell asked questions about her daily activities before the attack: whether she had noticed anything strange, how long she had been home, etcetera. Kala responded, careful not to say anything which would entice further accusations. She was sick of being accused.

She explained she always felt nervous and left the apartment only when necessary; the only time she had left in the two days before the attack was to get a coffee and four donuts from Dunkin Donuts. Boston Creme. She had developed a binge eating habit during anxiety days. Manic episodes often disoriented her, and she hated driving and being around people in those states. The emptiness inside formed a bottomless pit which she could not satisfy.

Detective Campbell confirmed the perpetrator performed maintenance at the apartment complex. He had a string of prior arrests; he was released each time on a technicality.

Kala wondered if he had a friend on the inside. How else could he be so lucky? There was something funny about Detective Shadow. She didn't trust him. It wasn't just the accusations either. She had felt a strong vibe from him; the sense was almost like the smell of gasoline just as it's been lit.

"The patient advocate is working to cancel your lease. You won't need to do anything, at least not just yet."

"Thank you for your help. Is there anything else you need?" Kala still wanted to show respect.

"That should be all. You can get the rest of the items from your apartment. I suggest you don't go yourself. It may not be the best idea."

"I already got what I need. Daniel went with me, after I received the call that my apartment was open. I must face my demons, not repress. I've repressed too long." She would no longer be a victim.

Detective Campbell and Detective Shadow left, a signed formal complaint in hand. Daniel hugged her and said, "Nice. Now that's over, let's relax." They spent a few weeks in Tennessee with Kala's family, then Kala went back to Minnesota with Daniel. She was with Daniel. She was home.

A few months later, they built a small house for themselves about an hour away from Kala's hometown. It was perfect for them, nestled in the woods with a long, curving driveway lined with towering evergreen trees for privacy. It was a two-story house built into a hill. They could climb on the roof from the back of the house with ease and watch the stars at night, cuddling in one another's arms as if they hadn't a care in the world.

The inside of the house was spacious but cozy, an upstairs office doubled as an art and music studio, and they had a home gym for the days when they couldn't hike outdoors. The living room was just down the hall, where Kala and Daniel practiced guitar and piano when they wanted to relax instead of recording their music. All in all, it was the perfect home for them.

Somehow, it was raised in a day when there were only a few people working. Women, at that. She suspected magic, although she wouldn't admit that to anyone, lest she be called crazy. Still, seeing strong women empowered Kala to be that fighter she longed to be, and she trained in Muay Thai again during times when she had too much energy. She wouldn't fight without cause, but she would fight for the greatest cause. Peace. Security. Freedom. Love. She had it all and hoped it would last this time.

3

I t was a summer night in Tennessee, four years after Kala's father had passed away. A bell chimed in her spirit each anniversary, an alarm that woke her from dreams, each more infuriating and confusing than the ones before. From experience, she knew the scenes would remain for hours—running, fighting and hiding from the same foes from her past. They haunted her, giving her no resolution.

Her body ached as if she had done the running and fighting in the waking world. Her insides hurt as if she had been tortured with endless unwanted sex. She hated having to deal with both the nightmares and grief, but they seemed to go hand in hand, as many of her traumas had happened around the same time. Her father had died six months after the worst of her personal traumas, when she needed his safety and warmth the most.

Why, after processing her memories, did she still ruminate about that attack? Was there a reason behind it? Was there meaning behind all the attacks?

She switched her mind; it was pointless to dwell on things she could not change. Her father wouldn't come back, and she would change—a short-sleeved t-shirt and jeans for the day—then she went into the living room and saw Daniel.

The positivity dam broke and she beamed at him. He was glorious, gifted, enticing, albeit cranky most days. She wanted to understand him to his core. She wanted to ease his mind.

He sat at the edge of his seat, acoustic guitar in hand, playing an altered version of her lullaby. He wrote it years before, while she slept in Afghanistan beside him. Her heart soared and would fly to the moon if she let it. She loved his creativity and compassion—when she wasn't toxic and ruining his calm. She tiptoed for a second, insecurities getting the better of her, but she squashed the urge once she recognized it. Right now he seemed calm, content, staring into the gray stone fireplace as he played.

He noticed her and gave a tight smile. His energy was neutral. Something was bothering him, but he didn't seem angry. A sadness filled his eyes, yet he showed no other outward signs of emotion. He would tell her in his own time; she needed to be calm and quiet so he could have the chance.

As she moved toward him, the heat of love washed over her, warming her body and spirit. She looked at the fireplace; the logs had burned to embers. She wondered when he had woken but didn't ask. She wanted to listen and absorb. Soft guitar notes flowed through the air, reminding her of his gentleness and comforting nature. Her shoulders relaxed a little, for she was home. Home. No matter where they went, she knew anywhere Daniel was would be her home. The thought warmed her more.

He watched her walk in, silent, hands never wavering from plucking the right notes. What was on his mind when he played that song? Would she ever know? How could he be so wonderful, so talented… and so mysterious? How could she feel love with just a look? His bright red hair highlighted his eyes, bluer than the cloudless noon sky and marbled with darker blue hues. She questioned why he loved her, and her looks. Her honey-blond hair paled in his red-gold light. Her own blue eyes paled compared to his. He was Daniel Blood, true to his name, and her twin flame.

"I love you," she blurted and rushed toward him with a smile so big she felt like the Joker. She stopped six inches in front of him and waited for him to let her know she wasn't crossing boundaries. Trying not to look impatient, she clasped her hands behind her back, much like parade rest in formation, but she had so much energy she twisted her core back and forth, warming her abdominals and back while she waited. At least her hyperactivity was multi-purposed.

He didn't make her wait or turn her away. She went in to hug him, but he intercepted, grabbing her hands in one of his, then booping her on the nose with his right index finger. She laughed and tried to boop him back. He dodged, and she attempted from another angle, pulling her head back in defense, reaching her arm toward him until she had retaliated the nose boop. She felt like *Stretch Armstrong;* she had wanted the stretchy action figure when she was young but had been the wrong gender to get one. She sobered at the thought, then he turned serious; the horseplay was over.

"I love you, too. How did you sleep?" He looked into her eyes, and she had to pull away before she burst into tears.

"I have no clue. Weird, that's how I slept. I think I had nightmares, but I'm too confused about them to tell whether they are... They feel real, like it will happen again."

"Kala, slow down. You're doing it again." His jaw clenched, but he did not react further. His eyes still showed love, but the irritable nature when he was dealing with sadness came in. They were alike in so many ways, but she could not get through to him when she needed to. How could she feel so lonely when she had felt at home just moments before? Darn emotional instabilities!

Kala shook her head and focused on Daniel. "What do you mean, 'I'm doing it again'? I'm just communicating my feelings to you."

"You're confusing the fuck out of me. Reset." He turned around, picked up his guitar, and put it in its case. It was ready for the trip.

Her body shook, a deep, hollow sensation in the pit of her stomach. She had overwhelmed him... again. He felt her pain already; she didn't need to tell him every time she was stressed. And if she was confused in her own head, how confused did she make him? She clasped her hands together and hung her head. "Sorry, it's been a long time since I bothered you like that. Something is wrong, my brain isn't working properly. I have a sense of deja vu."

"Nope, you're wrong. We had this issue a couple of nights ago." His eyes seemed wary. "Are you witchy again?"

A red light flashed behind her eyes and nothing existed for a moment. It was over so quickly; she didn't think anything until Daniel asked where she was. "I'm in the living room, with you, Daniel. Where else would I be?"

"I don't... never mind. What do you think is wrong?"

"Anxiety, I think. I'm not sure. It's hard to describe. I... I feel like I'm waiting for something to happen. My spirit feels... trapped. Or... I don't know... like it's trying to escape from me." Another breath. "Maybe I'm just nervous about our adventure. You haven't told me what we're doing."

He smiled a sad smile that held a hint of intrigue. It was endearing... and frustrating. How long until he trusted her enough to talk to her about whatever bothered him? Or, maybe it was a good mystery.

A spark ignited something inside her. Would he propose? They only packed food and survival items for camping. Maybe critters would welcome them into their homes? Maple seeds helicoptered in her belly until they hit bottom and hope emerged as if the tree grew inside her. Rooting her to the ground, to the air, to the wind, to life. The red light came back, a sign she would disconnect from reality soon, and she saw a cardinal in a tree; its war cry drew her attention. A tear drop sapphire ring sat atop an acorn to the right of it. Daniel spoke to a squirrel. It retrieved the ring and the acorn and climbed on her shoulder to place the ring atop her hand. It was up to her to choose—put it on or decline. She would always choose Daniel. She had to force her mind back to reality, but the idea was cute in her mind.

Daniel moved to the chair, across from the fireplace. Kala moved, too, sitting in front of him on the floor to feel his warmth against her back and on her sides. She was safe with him. And knew she always would be. Sighing, she lay her head on his knee.

His fingers brushed the straggling hair from her forehead and cheek. They were gentle yet strong. Calloused from years of working with his hands and learning the instruments that brought magic into their lives. Another rush of excitement. How could one person be so right for her, even with their problems? The tree inside her swayed, churning the bile and stomach acids which had no food to digest.

"Kala, we need to talk."

Those dreaded words. His calves tensed against her. His energy changed, too. She became more nervous as his nervousness increased; would they fight? The last time they fought, they canceled their plans and almost their lives. They almost always canceled their plans; too much fear. Stupid fear.

"There's something I need to tell you." Daniel's voice shook.

Kala turned around to face Daniel then changed her mind and sat on the couch next to his chair. She sat sideways with her back against the cool leather armrest—it soothed her aching mid-back a bit. She planted her feet on the couch, knees bent. She needed to move, but she wouldn't show it. She would sit and be patient, not interrupt. Memories of her trying to stay still while her father taught her to fish popped into her mind. Her thumb and middle finger tapped together against her leg. She growled under her breath then focused back on him.

"Okay, I'm ready. I needed to prepare myself. I just miss Daddy… I wish he was still here." She had felt alone and scared ever since her father's death. Now she only felt a connection with Daniel.

"Breathe, Kala. It will be okay… but I haven't been honest with you. Do you remember last year, when we were apart?"

Kala tensed at the mention and noticed Daniel was worried too. No matter what, she would always forgive him. He couldn't do anything to cause her to doubt their love. "Yes." Then she held her breath without intending to. A fleeting thought, barely registered, flew by in the whirlwind of her thoughts. *Less work equals less energy expended during stressful times.* It was her mind preserving energy.

"A year ago, a man came to visit me in Minnesota. He knew you weren't home and asked me not to tell you until today, his fourth death anniversary." Kala said nothing but squinted her eyes and turned her head like a confused puppy. Daniel put his hand on her leg and said in a hoarse, cracking voice, "Your father is alive."

"What? That's... impossible. If it were true..." Kala couldn't utter it, the unthinkable. Tears streamed down her face and her nose dripped. "I need a tissue. Perfect time for me to break down, right when I need to think."

Her moves were abrupt, chaotic. She seethed at herself. Reality distorted, tempting her to jump in a distant, dark crater in the back of her mind while blocking her way back to the world with a wavy veil—one she could not penetrate. Nothing made sense to her. She groped for the wall, chair—anything that would connect her to that moment, to Daniel and the warmth. Cold penetrated to her marrow, dragging her into the abyss.

Embrace the chaos. Release. Breathe. Aaram. She smiled, noticing the language differences bring her mind back. *Aaram*, the Persian-Dari word for calm; that's what she would be. Calm chaos.

Daniel handed her a tissue and an ice pack. She gave a weak smile and thanked him; he smiled with tears in his eyes and hugged her tight. She melted into him and tried to quiet the senses.

Extraneous stimuli in all varieties—sight, sound, feeling, even taste. The smell of a nickel after it's been touched, a migraine symptom of hers, filled her nostrils and curdled her tongue until she gasped, needing something acidic to take it away. She groped her way to the refrigerator and gulped straight from the orange juice bottle. It was almost empty; she would need to get more.

Daniel followed her into the kitchen, standing close and watching her with his hand out, as if to catch her if she fell. She could see something—an emerald green light shining around him. His tone was serious, but the love was there. "It's true. I will prove it. But first..."

Kala giggled at his words, her childish mind taking over to calm her. Daniel raised an eyebrow.

"You said butt first... Tee–hee," she said as she put the orange juice away and stuck her tongue out at him.

"Kala, you're silly." He laughed with her—it was enough to bring her further into the moment.

"What's your proo—?" Her vocal cords interrupted with excited spasms. She blushed.

"Wait here. And..." He walked away without finishing the sentence, a habit which might have made her laugh if she wasn't so jittery.

"What else were you saying?"

"Oh, I have this for you, too." He pulled something from his pocket. As She reached out tentative fingers, he hesitated. Her eyes were drawn back to his. "No matter what, I want you to be happy and safe. And I will be there for you... I had this made for you. It has special properties."

Kala opened her hand, wondering what properties something that fitted in a pocket could have. Her thought turned to wonder. He held out a ring, identical to the one she had imagined. Or had she imagined it? Reality and dreams collided, and she couldn't be certain she hadn't seen it in their home by mistake.

She examined the ring in his hand. The tear-drop sapphire reminded her of her unstable emotions yet it sparkled, light travelled through it—her birthstone fit her personality. It was a translucent navy blue, high quality, with a silver band inlaid with diamonds.

How had she known? *Had* she seen it and not recognized what it was? Maybe that was it. She could have seen it and blocked it because her mind was racing. That wasn't something new. She forgot a lot of things. All the time. Maybe she could track down the memory's whereabouts.

"Do you hate it?"

"NO! That's not it at all! I have deja vu, or rather, I pictured that ring being presented to me by a squirrel. A cardinal alerted me to it. I still have trouble not feeling psychic when things like this happen."

Daniel's other eyebrow raised, going higher each second. "Are you calling me squirrely?" His sculpted face showed shock, yet a sparkle in his eyes gave him away.

She laughed, grabbing the ring with such enthusiasm she could have ripped his hand from his wrist. "If you're squirrely, I'm the squirrely queen and you're the squirrely king." She went to put the ring on her left hand and raised a questioning eyebrow to him. "This is a proposal, right? You want to marry me, not just be my bodyguard?"

Daniel became serious again. Marine mode. "No, you got me. I only want to beat people up for you." They both laughed, then he said, "We still have a lot to work out, but I want us to have hope, a life together." His eyes pleaded with her to understand, and she did.

She could sense his enthusiasm—his sadness, fear… every emotion, even a little resentment—showing in that one statement and his energy. She felt the same. Life was too unpredictable to hope for a relationship to last with their issues. They had to be sure.

Yet something held her back from true understanding. Details. Connections. How did Daniel keep that secret from her without her knowing he was hiding something? She trusted him, that's how. And she didn't regret it. He had told her when he was able. A promise was a promise, and broken promises lead to broken relationships.

But what had happened during the last four years? If her father was alive, she needed to know how, why… and why he had never told her himself. "I need to know everything, please."

The energy changed in the room; another was added. A familiar one, which seemed to meld with both Kala's and Daniel's energies. She felt stronger, whole.

"We don't have time." Kala's father's voice echoed through the room and into her soul.

Kala jumped and turned around. Instead of seeing the room, she saw the red light behind her eyes. This time, the disconnect stayed while she gasped for air that wouldn't come. Her soul tried to escape her body again, the stress was too much, but she caught it just in time and stopped it from fleeing. She needed to see, to know. If he was alive…? Hope and sorrow filled her, but she did not care. The truth. That's what she wanted. And she wouldn't settle until she felt the truth was her own.

But what if this was all a dream? What if she awoke, after all this hope, to find herself alone, in turmoil? She couldn't bear it; she couldn't face it.

She went from suspicious to shameful to scared to accepting, talking to herself aloud with each emotion. She paced the room and pulled at her shirt, picked at her nails, clenched every muscle in her body as she panicked. Kala felt her legs bruise as she walked into the edges of tables and sofas, unable to see past the red behind her eyes yet unable to stop moving.

Tears alternated with laughter; not soft, eccentric. Grabbing balance was like chasing the Tasmanian Devil in circles. She laughed harder when she thought of how she must look.

No wonder Daniel called her Taz. She was a tornado, cycling hot and cold breath until it destroyed the fear in its path. The shame that came with false obligation filled her until she wanted to scream. Instead, she sighed, feeling the breeze on her face. Where did it come from? Inside her mind? Who cared? It was there, bringing her peace. Calm peeked its head in long enough for her to say, "I need a minute."

After seconds rather than a minute, she looked at James, straight into his eyes, her voice a whisper. "Daddy?"

She burst into tears again, this time not caring if she slimed. She needed to hug him, to tackle and bear hug. Bear hugs he would give her when she was sad as a child would always help. It was like she was five again and her father lived. It was odd to think of, but she had hope.

As he hugged her, she assessed the energy and emotions in the air and on faces, wanting to understand, to heal, to grow together so they could change for the better. After five years of therapies, failures, dialectical behavior practice, and being with someone who reminded her to focus on the present, she still had trouble staying sane.

Her father seemed the same as he did in her dreams, although there were some differences. Only a part of him was here.

Something was missing. Trying to put herself in his shoes, she assessed—a father needing to bond with his daughter, for the first time in four years? Why hadn't he called or written, stopped by for lunch? She knew he missed her when she was a child and he drove eighteen-wheelers; he would send postcards or even take her with him. He was working then, and she always knew where he was, that he cared. But why leave her when she needed to hear his voice the most? Had her instability toward others pushed him away too?

She had even gone to his funeral and written him a letter in Dari, the language she had learned in the military, which she hoped he could read—at least when she had believed in Heaven. Inside his coffin, she had also placed a Care Bear balloon, signifying she would always be his Kalabear.

It didn't matter that he had abandoned her. He now wanted to make amends, and she welcomed it. But why now? When she'd finally figured out some things in her life? And how had he faked his death? He had been so weak, unable to talk without a computer, before he died. At least that's what she recalled.

"I'm sorry... so sorry." He hugged her tighter. His warm energy caused her to snuggle against his shoulder. The love was there and would never leave. She felt like a child once more.

He had lost weight, no longer had his *pregnant belly,* their inside joke. She remembered his illness had given him edema, but it was undiagnosed for years. But now she could get her arms around him. He released his hold a little, treating her like a porcelain doll.

"What's wrong?" Kala wiped her eyes and looked up at him, mouth-breathing a little, wiping at her stuffy nose.

She looked closer, analyzing every detail she could distinguish through the void in her mind. His eyes looked almost empty, the same light blue as hers, but little light or life in them. His honey blond hair seemed dull and unkempt, like he didn't care. His eyebrows were as long, salt-and-peppered, and messy as she recalled, but she couldn't smile.

He didn't seem happy to see her, or as happy as she was, and that scared her. Was he still sick? Was she a bad person? That's what she had been told during her marriage, but she didn't believe it. Or did she?

"We are in danger, especially you." With one more quick squeeze, he pushed her out of the embrace and turned away. "We have to go now. Have you packed?"

Kala froze, not daring to move. His stern look mirrored the one he used to give her all those years ago. He had taken her on the road with him and would tell her to stay put while he went to the restroom. He wouldn't even let other women take her to the bathroom with them; instead, she would stand sentry over herself, telling men her father would kick their butts if they touched her. Where was the version of him that told her things would be okay? A heaviness filled her stomach, burying the tree which was there moments ago. She could say nothing, for she was nothing.

"Yes," Daniel said, glancing over as he did something she couldn't quite see. He handed Kala her shoes and jacket; his hiking boots were on his feet, and a water-resistant hooded jacket covered the bag.

Feeling as though she did something to be pushed away by them both, Kala's shoulders sunk as she grappled with her shoelaces then grabbed her bag and copied Daniel's idea. If they were fleeing on foot, they would need rain protection. But why would they flee on foot? That was ridiculous.

Then she had no words, again no being. This time, the chatter was gone. She could escape the pain. The constant noise, analysis, everything. Nothing would make sense until she had some time to process, so she would wait. But when would that be?

"Daddy, please tell me what's going on. The short version will work, but why did you fake your death, why did you stay away from me, and why must we flee?"

He smiled at her, a warm expression that brought some of the life into his eyes. "I'm sorry I had to lie to you. I will tell you more later, but know that part of me did die, and you would have been in danger had I stayed. A group called the Qazanat wants you for a reason I can't understand, and they want me to harm you. I refused, so they held me prisoner until I could escape. They could have harmed you through me. I would not let that happen."

She didn't quite understand, but she trusted him. She would go with her two protectors, her caregiver and her love who had helped her grow. She could do this; she could practice situational awareness despite the fear.

A click in her mind and she was in the Void, a shell of herself, content in being there for Daniel and her father, but no other emotion. She had not figured out what caused this Void in her, but she understood it as a protective mechanism. She didn't need to worry; she needed to focus. If they were happy with her, she could be happy, or at least feel like she did something right. *But why would an organization be after her?*

The wavy veil protected her psyche from the terror and she just… existed as an onlooker, living a vicarious life through an organic-grown robot body.

In the back of her mind, buried beyond the reach of conscious and subconscious thought, a hidden part of her whispered to remember the past.

★ ☾ ☀ ★

The night air was cool as they walked away from the house. Dew had already formed on the grass below their feet, darkening her hiking boots. She could feel the cold through her socks. She hadn't been wearing socks before. And she had worn pajamas the last time she had checked. When had she changed her clothes? Lost in thought, she hadn't seen the changes around her, but she felt them. Two energies pulled against each other, like trying to close a door during a windstorm. It didn't feel right. It felt... forced.

When she looked ahead, she stopped and wondered if insanity had taken her. The usual gravel streets and houses didn't exist. She couldn't see or hear any cars. The forest from her childhood home was ahead, a path surrounded by trees, leading to tiny waterfalls and springs in the distance. She had loved hiking in her backyard growing up.

It didn't make sense. "Wait, Daddy. Where are we? It looks like where we used to live, but that's an hour away! What's going on?"

He turned to look toward her. The patient look didn't leave his eyes yet he whispered urgently, "It's a portal. I'm not sure how it works, Kalabear, but it connects twin worlds to one another. I've been told that a connection with you allows me to travel through it; you must be the key to accessing other worlds. If we do not go to Derowa, the magical twin to Earth's logical world, humanity is doomed."

Kala craned her neck to hear him, but his words spoke volumes to her. She had often thought she belonged in another world, a world in her head. Perhaps her disconnection from reality was an out of body experience—she had practiced that skill through meditations just to see if she could connect with her Daddy's spirit. Good thinking if this was evasion. She needed to remember everything she had learned during her military and therapy training and maintain focus. Quiet movements, look, see, feel, hear...

experience. She would be one with nature so she could tell any differences. She closed her eyes to focus on breathing then said, "Will we be safe on the other side?"

"No, we will be in more danger. But I promise you're ready to cross and it must be now." After a moment, he looked straight at her and said, "I don't deserve your trust, but I'm asking for it." His eyes became a blue crystal lake; she could drown in the sadness they evoked. She wanted to trust him and she believed in his goodness.

"I trust you." She hoped he would let her know when it was safe, but she wanted to figure that out on her own as well. She would remember what she learned in therapy and focus on the present. No matter what, they would all survive. She would see to it.

James led them into the forest and Kala followed Daniel. Occasionally he looked back to give a reassuring smile. She welcomed the smile, but the forest distracted her. She couldn't push it out.

It seemed the night sounds shook the earth beneath their feet. Owls hooted from treetops when the team stepped on rocks, and crickets chirped from the ground when leaves fell. The moon shone amid the forest, illuminating areas prone to shadow.

As they trekked uphill, the leaves began to melt, dripping hot sludge onto Kala's shoulder, churning to mush beneath her feet. A cold pain seeped into her soul. The further they traveled into the forest, the more she feared the worst. Everything would fail. She would keep failing until there was nothing left to strive for. She would die alone so fear could reign supreme.

The sudden odd quiet intensified her doubts. A constant cold pain stabbed behind her right eye, which blurred in a way that doubled her vision. Her insides moved as if she was on a boat. She didn't have her sea legs; the ship carrying her sense of self would be wrecked.

She looked down. Instead of water, congealed blood stuck to her feet and climbed her legs. It was heavy, like the blood of every person, living or dead, holding her down when she needed to get free. Down, down, legs giving in under the weight of sludge on her shoulders. The blood crept to her scalp faster than she could breathe. She would be low crawling soon, then she would suffocate in the muck. She would not give up. She had to follow James and Daniel. They would need her.

"Kala? Can you hear me?"

Daniel? Where was he, why couldn't she see him? Two handsome, identical faces appeared, bending over her.

"You blacked out."

She was on the ground. Something tickled the back of her head. She could feel the heat in it, a stinging wound, the tingling of her nerves, and she could smell the blood. She wanted to lick it, preserve it, get it back in her body. *What was that thought?* Daniel still searched her eyes for some reassurance. "I think I had a panic attack, but I'm not sure." *Was it all in my head?*

James walked back to them, leaves crunching under his feet. "I didn't expect this. There's something wrong here. It feels different. They couldn't have, could they?" He looked back and forth, panic showing on him.

"Couldn't have what? Who? *What's going on?*"

"Stop yelling," Daniel said. His face, redder than she had ever seen it, showed a throbbing vein on the temple. It would burst if he wasn't careful. "There's something out there. Listen."

Kala pulled feeble breaths as she strained to hear through the constant ringing in her ears. She growled and dug her fingernails into her forearm. The pain brought her back to the moment. She had regained control over her body. Fear would not be her master anymore.

"Here," said an eerie voice; chills surged through Kala's spine. The rustling leaves echoed throughout the cosmos. She stood to run but fell instead. The ground seemed to melt underneath her and glued her to the spot. She couldn't move, do anything, not even hear. Death was there for her and she would submit.

She was back in the room at SERE school in two-thousand-five, when she had been plied with alcohol and told there was a get-together with the rest of the group.

No… *Not the time for a flashback…*

A man walked over to her—she was under his spell. His balding head dripped sweat, which rolled down his chubby, pock-marked face. Brown, sewage-colored eyes locked with hers and his eyes smiled more each time she showed fear. She tried to show none but her fingers gave her away. Thump, thump, thump…

He pushed her down on the bed, held her down as he stabbed with his fingers. A scratch. And another. He tore into her until she was wet with blood before he changed his tactic. Hurting her wasn't enough; he needed to destroy her.

The more she cried, the more excited he became. He relished her pain, and she loathed his existence. She had wanted him dead. She would do it with her hands. Rip his throat out like a wolf, taste his blood, proving he lived no more.

He did not use protection; he could pass anything to her. It was done for him. For her, it would never be over. She lay there, no longer an innocent; tainted. She looked toward him to search for signs of humanity, but none showed. He didn't even look at her.

He talked to others instead. Some looked at her with eager eyes, others were hesitant, even showing sympathy. But sympathy wouldn't last. Without warning, at least twenty other men approached and reveled in their sexual feast, taking away everything she valued, everything she was. They did destroy her. She wanted it to end, all of it. She would do whatever it took.

"NO! I will not yield again!"

She was back in the present. It had been four and a half years since that attack, yet the memories seemed more real than the present world she lived in. She had been fooled and led to believe she *was* a fool. She had accepted an invitation into his room, thinking a group would be there with her. She had just wanted to sleep off the alcohol they had plied her with, but a nagging voice had told her it would be rude to reject the invitation.

Damn it, I was so stupid! The group had been sent off beforehand and she had believed her attacker's lies. No more!

She breathed into her diaphragm, the air filling her belly and giving her life. If magic was real, what could she do? She could save herself and others ... or could she?

Glowing blue fire erupted around her, encircling her, protecting her from harm. The fire emitted heat at its edges, yet was cold in her hands, light and darkness, stable chaos. She would survive this ordeal, become stronger in the end. She had to get away.

Even with the freedom fire, she began to feel woozy. Each step she took was agony—her right ankle swelled with the force as she attempted to remove it from the soil. How had the earth melted in the cool but not when the fire she wove blazed hotter than hot as it expanded from her in a wave? She couldn't imagine what could cause such a conundrum.

Wait, what am I doing? How was she doing this? Was it... magic? Was she the Devil? No, it couldn't be. She wanted to *save* people from harm, not cause them harm. The Devil wouldn't want people to be safe.

She let go of her sense of urgency. The fires dropped, became embers as the whirlwind slowed. Where each fell, the earth began to stabilize until she could get free. She ran. A few flames still surrounded her, but it wouldn't last. She wasn't safe. She had to get away.

She looked back for Daniel and James; they weren't there. She had to go back for them. Survivor's guilt would be worse than the fear she had; she knew this from experience.

She turned around and sprinted back uphill, ready to face the beings she felt but couldn't see. They had the same energy as her flashbacks, rancid and decaying, yet there was also a strange connection between them and herself. She looked at them for the first time.

They looked like demons. Their greying, bumpy skin blended in with the shadows. Who knew what powers they could have? She couldn't get away from them. Maybe they would barter. Could demons be trusted? She focused harder. Somehow, she could sense they were once human. Not hostile, not friendly. Unknowns. *Maybe* she could talk to them.

The creatures she could see didn't blink. Glowing emerald eyes watched her with curiosity. They were a stark contrast to skin that looked like bubbling grey tar. Charcoal grey scales lined their brow and traveled down their noses. For a reason she couldn't fathom, she was reminded of the Ninja Turtles.

Her body vibrated as she held her ground—she was a volcano, waiting to erupt. It was strange. What were these creatures, and why did they just stand there? The energies of more than twenty beings surrounded her, some blending into the trees—hidden, but not to her senses.

She had no alternative. Kala took a breath and asked, "What do you want?" The creatures looked back and forth toward each other. Had she surprised them?

"We want you to come with us," the tallest of the creatures said in a gravelly voice that echoed through the dense trees.

"What do you want with me?"

"We do what our master says. He needs you; you *will* come with us."

"What if I refuse?"

"They will die where they lay." She looked at James and Daniel, both on the ground. Something was amiss. Daniel's hair dulled with each second and he tossed in his sleep. James sat silent against a tree. His eyes moved and showed fear, but he had not changed in appearance.

"Let them live and I will come with you."

"We promise." The creature had something in its hand. Checkmate was inevitable. "Take this. You cannot be awake when we cross or you will become like us."

Shivering, Kala took the bottle from the creature and opened a tonic which looked and smelled like vodka. Her stomach heaved with force. Images tried to resurface, but she squashed them. *Why do they care if I get their disease? Why do I feel I can trust them? There's something... odd about their energies. It feels like... me.* "Do you have anything different?"

"No. Take it."

"I'll just puke it up. I'd rather stay conscious. I'll risk becoming whatever you are. Here." She handed the bottle back to the creature, who stared at her as though she were insane. Perhaps she was. Guilt for being rude battled with the knowledge they were kidnapping her. Why was she so willing to accept this behavior? There was something familiar about these creatures, something calming. It bothered her to trust them yet she couldn't think of anything else to do. "Let me say goodbye."

She kissed James and Daniel each on the cheek, whispering in her head that she would rejoin them even if she didn't survive. She had to be brave; Daniel couldn't always protect her, but their bond was what allowed her to access her powers, she was sure of it.

"I love you both." She adjusted the sapphire ring on her finger, feeling its protection from fear. She felt peace knowing she had love in her life. "I'm only leaving to protect you. May this sacrifice truly protect you from harm. This isn't over—please, please, please... remember that. I will find a way back to you." *Alive or dead.*

Giving a hug to each of them while they lay on the ground, she felt the weight of her decision. Something inside her feared the worst—she had abandoned them. It was a pain she didn't want to inflict on anyone, let alone the two men who had helped her most.

She took three deep breaths and left with her intriguing captors, walking through a dark hole that seemed a rip in the world itself. The jagged lines around the portal echoed with pain and torture. Her subconscious took a picture.

She would at least recall this emotion. Hope and grief. Fear and love. Balance. *I can deal with that.*

5

K ala attempted nonchalance and confidence when walking through the portal, which was darker than night. She stumbled a few times but feigned strength. She had a sense these creatures could see in the dark.

Standing upright was difficult. A heaviness threatened to consume her if she looked around. Even when she fell, she kept her eyes forward. What would become of them all? She could feel Daniel and James with them. Were they collateral or necessary for whatever quest she would take? *This is an adventure, a quest. If I don't see it as that, I will fail.*

A strange, blinding light loomed at the end of the portal. She shielded her eyes with one hand, trying to stop the needles in her corneas; her right eye hurt the most. When her vision cleared, she saw the most wonderous image. Water extended in front of them, and a stone bridge led to a mansion in the distance that appeared to be made of water, waves towering above her head. She couldn't be sure yet they appeared to be within transparent cases. "Where are we?"

thing; it had already happened to these sad people. Her heart sank, and she wondered if she could be happy again. It was a stupid thought, but it was survival. What could she do to remain happy when everyone wanted to keep her down? She would practice the skills she had been taught in therapy and which she knew secondhand in peaceful situations. How would they compare?

She tried to turn back but the mutant stopped her. She felt weird for thinking of them as a mutant. "I don't mean to be offensive, but what are you? I've never seen anything or anyone like you." Something in her mind told her he wouldn't harm her, at least not willingly. She just felt it in her gut.

The creature looked at his cohorts before turning back to Kala. Their strange eyes still glowed bright. "We are... Qurban, compelled to obey the Master of Blood."

Master of Blood? What kind of creepy name was that? What had she gotten herself into? Always running in head-first without knowledge or a plan.

Her eyes roamed while the Qurban led her down a corridor which looked like a flowing stream under a leaking transparent surface, though cracks were not visible. She wanted to reach through the surface and feel the smooth stones on its bed, collect them and call them her own. Come to think of it, the entire building, Terois Manor—one would almost call it a castle—rippled and was water-like. Abeja, the land of water, they had said.

Could it be magic? Of course, magic. She wondered again if she was dreaming but stopped wondering once they stopped in front of a door.

A rancid energy emanated from the room, one she recognized, though it had been years since she had felt it. The rapist was back for more. Would she freeze this time, or would she run, or fight? She wanted to do the latter, and told her brain as much, yet her confidence waned as the door opened. Sewage-brown eyes smiled at her, delighting in her fear which overwhelmed every sense of herself. Carl Arresto, the man who had stolen her world. Now she would die, inside if not out.

Kala stood her ground, refused to budge when the Qurban pushed her inside. "It will be easier if you don't fight," the Qurban said through sad, glowing eyes which shed heavy, gel-like tears. How did that dense tear push through the duct? It looked impossible; it also looked painful.

"*Look at me!*" Carl bellowed. Kala directed her attention back at him and realized something. She no longer feared him. He looked pathetic. His pock-marked face reddened with anger, and his dull brown hair did not cover his round head. He began to resemble a hideous red and brown spotted dog creature, throwing a tantrum because it couldn't eat the rug.

Laughter burst from Kala's mouth. "Wow, you haven't changed much over the years, except gaining more weight and losing more hair." She hoped he wouldn't suffocate her with that weight again. Fat chance of avoiding it.

Carl backhanded Kala. Stars formed in her vision and she blinked. She reached toward her face, feeling the indentations of a ring; two round marks which left a tainted energy in her skin. The rest of her face felt the stinging heat of that slap. She massaged the marks with intention to reduce inflammation she knew would come soon.

When he was done, Kala looked down at her toes to get her bearings. As she wiggled them, she realized something else. She knew how to deal with torturers. She had done it her whole life. Behind her protective screen, she could accept what was happening and plan an escape... or vengeance.

In the moment, she was leaning more toward vengeance, but anger was a horrible emotion to rely upon; it always left marks on the aggressor. She couldn't be impulsive. A few breaths and she was ready to look at him again.

"No matter what you do, you won't break me again. I won't let you. So, *peshey jehnam bero!*" The words were out of her mouth before she could stop them. *Go to hell* was what she had said, only in a rough Afghani way.

The Qurban looked at her with surprise. "How do you know our language?"

Their language? It was a language in Afghanistan, and this wasn't Afghanistan, or even Earth.

"You!" Carl pointed at the Qurban. "Shut your mouth. Don't talk to her again, that's an order!" He twisted the tainted ring on his finger as he said this. The Qurban who had spoken remained silent, though his lips quivered as if he wanted to say more. Kala's eyes zoomed in on the ring.

Two odd-shaped orbs filled with a ruby liquid-like substance shimmered in a strange, dark way. Kala had never seen anything like it; how could something shimmer with darkness? Still, she saw it. Even more bizarre was the embellishing. Mercuric handcuffs that somehow held their shape instead of oozing locked around each orb. A conical red stone she could not identify sat upon each of the orbs.

Her stomach lurched; she interpreted it as a symbol of sex trafficking and death of an identity. Was it happening again, like it had in her marriage? The unfamiliar world spun for ages before all went dark. She could take no more.

"Wake up, you lazy whore! I'm not done with you yet."

Kala breathed in then sputtered as salted ice water splashed over her, stinging wounds Kala did not remember getting. She looked down, longing to know what had happened, scared to know how it would affect her in the long run. She was bound, hands and feet tied behind a hard surface, one that scraped her bare skin. She looked up to see a jagged spike of coral; looking down, she saw it jutting from a greenish-black tile floor, one which didn't fit the décor of Terois Manor. The tiles had a hungry vibe to them. What did they eat?

Every inch of her seemed covered in bruises and she could tell a few bones were either bruised, cracked, or broken. Her ribs screamed for mercy every time she breathed, and her pelvis ached as if it had been spread apart for too long. Her insides felt raw. She was a mess. An angered mess.

"Look at me, you stupid whore!" Carl's screams squeaked a little as he became angrier. She wanted to laugh, as she saw anger as the opposite of confident; confidence demanded a mindful approach, one without screaming.

She wouldn't let anger win. Her own anger turned to curiosity, and with that curiosity she would prevail. Her wrists writhed as she clenched her fists and flexed her fingers. Whatever held her wrists in place didn't budge, even enough for her to dislocate her thumb to get loose. She would have to find another way.

Carl had been walking around, trying to intimidate her, but she blocked the fear with her protective screen. She wouldn't let him win, not again. Every failed attempt to get free heightened that sense of foreboding. She stopped moving, feeling like a mouse in a trap. She waited for the rattlesnake to come and gobble her up.

Carl released her hands and feet with a wave of his hand, and she fell to the floor. Ignoring the pain, she stood. Carl kicked her legs out from under her. He kicked a few more times, aiming at her injured bones. She curled into the fetal position to protect her internal organs and breathed through the pain. *I can't let him win. He will not break my will to live... not again.*

Her insides screamed, white-hot light spilled from around her right eye, the pain inside subsiding as it flowed. When the light surrounded them on all sides, Carl reared back and slapped Kala, her blood spattering around her and on her naked body. She watched as the floor absorbed what blood touched it. The floor's hungry vibes intensified; its energy seemed to reach for more.

She swallowed a glare, ready to survive without emotion. Only wisdom from the emotion would be used. She needed more information before she could plan an escape.

"Look at me, slut." His voice seemed menacing on the outside, but Kala could see he was getting desperate. But why?

She wouldn't poke the bear, but the bear needed to stop, lest it lose its life. She was close to a willingness to kill again to get away. She gazed right at the bastard, focusing her angry energy into the white lights which zoomed toward him, coming at his heart from all sides. He gasped. He landed hard on his back—it popped, and his breath became shallow.

Kala stood and darted past Carl, rubbing her wrists and limping in a half-run. He groaned as he grabbed at her foot and pulled. She lost her balance for a moment but pushed herself upright and ran faster towards the door, feet sliding in the blood on the dark tiles, blood which they consumed more of with each second.

Luck was with her; Carl was still on the floor. She looked around. There were no windows, only the door straight ahead. It looked like she would have to navigate enemy territory for a while, moving like a ninja, like she had practiced most of her life.

The door opened in front of her and the Qurban stopped her, an apology in his eyes. From behind her, Carl screamed, "Take her to the Void! Give her the potion and bring back her fear!" The Void sounded like a lame cartoon weapon, but a potion? What would it do to her? How would they bring back her fear? She could see they didn't want to obey Carl; their eyes showed sadness instead of excitement. She didn't hesitate to follow the Qurban.

She needed to cooperate; she wasn't strong enough to take them on without help. She could now sense a strength in them, a strength that wasn't there when they had first met. Strange… Carl seemed much weaker than he had all those years ago. Was she stronger, or had he weakened since the event?

While she walked, she assessed her memories of the event. How had she done the magic and what did it do? Annoy him, most likely. He seemed to have a compulsion power; she would have to learn more about herself, about her powers, and resist his compulsions.

He had tortured her at SERE. But she still knew what to do. Survive, Evade, Resist, Escape. Too bad he had had the same survival training as her.

* ☾ ☼ *

There was so much Kala didn't understand, but she still held her head as high as the pain would allow her. She refused to limp, to groan, or to cry. She would appear confident, like she'd learned in therapy and basic military training. Her military bearing had surprised everyone in SERE. Perhaps she could win this battle of wills. How long would she be held captive? What was happening to Daniel and to her father?

Each of the Qurban nodded as they passed her, two led the way while the other two guarded behind her. She thought about potential obstacles to her escape. Infections and unhealed bones could be detrimental to escape. Could she bathe? Probably not, based on her treatment so far. Still, she would remain strong and as focused as she could. She made her long neck stretch toward the heavens and pulled her shoulder blades back and down, a relaxation technique she had practiced in yoga. She could ignore the pains for a time—physical and mental alike.

The pace down the maze-like halls was so slow, Kala tripped over her own toes. Every so often, she flat tired the Qurban in front of her, especially if he stopped to let someone else pass. His broken sandals thwacked on the coral-like rocks sticking up from the water floor, which dug into Kala's naked feet. It seemed the corridors stretched for ages, only to drop down to another level via chutes, ramps, and ladders that looked out of place and new.

There was so much stimulation, she had a hard time focusing on her walk and lost her footing each time she saw women or young girls being led like cattle. They were also naked, covered in bruises, and bleeding from multiple areas. She wished she could rub her ring for peace but all her clothes, jewelry, and gear had been missing when she woke up in Carl's room.

"Why are there only women and little girls here?" Her lip remained curled in open disgust, especially when she saw young girls bleeding when they were too young for it.

"You ask strange questions. None about yourself. Why?"

Kala said nothing in response but began to feel what had happened to her, and the physical pain dimmed in comparison to the pain in her soul. She couldn't think. She needed rest. Yet she knew rest would not come. Not as a prisoner of some war between herself and nearly every man she had encountered. She needed Daniel and James. Only then would she be safe.

No, she must be safe without them. He would not be able to help her in his current condition. She would help him instead. Why had he fainted around the Qurban? He was so much stronger than her…

Every step was agony, but Kala focused on scanning around her, feeling that everyone stared at her. She had always stood out, no matter where she went. It was too much. She had to get out of here, and she had to get these women and children out. She didn't even like the way the Qurban were treated; she could see they hadn't chosen this life. They would all be free. And then they could stop the Qazanat, whoever they were. They had to defeat these jerks for anyone to have peace. The flame in her head ignited brighter than she imagined, and she tried to send some of the light to others. They would all need it to survive, resist, and escape this hell.

Soon the Qurban stopped. Every muscle acknowledged it by tensing, putting extra pressure behind her right eye. What lay ahead?

Well, for one thing, there didn't seem to be a door. But she could see darkness beyond the water-tiles; it seemed to block the way. The lead Qurban hesitated then nodded. A Qurban pushed her through, and the world was black once more.

James gritted his teeth, seething, as Carl laughed. "I told you she would be mine. One day, she will obey me without force."

"She will never choose your side. There's too much good in her. Her light will defeat your darkness."

Carl laughed again; spittle flew onto James' face. James' hands, tied behind his back, flexed as if they wanted to wipe it away. His stomach heaved as he smelt Carl's sickly breath.

"You will see." Carl crooked his finger towards one of the guards. "Keep him chained in the viewing room. Don't let him miss any of my victories."

Searing pain erupted between James' eyes. The compulsion power from Carl reminded him of the time before he quit smoking, when he had burned himself with a cigarette. He could almost hear the voice of Carl's compulsion. *Hurt, maim, kill, you will do what I say.*

James closed his eyes, focusing on the pain in his head; as he breathed, he imagined himself in a boat on a lake, fishing for dinner with his family. The pain reduced to a simmer then fled, leaving a dull ache in its place. Carl wasn't his master, God was. God represented love, not pain.

A guard pushed James to the corner of Carl's office. Terois Manor had changed since he was first brought here, four years ago. At that point, the manor had been a stronghold for Abeja; no one had penetrated its walls in hundreds of years.

Now the sickly energies and misdeeds of the Qazanat permeated the water where James had felt the most at home in Derowa. A naval sea captain at heart, he missed the open ocean, where he was free to smell fresh air unpolluted by society.

The guard pressed an arrow into a taxidermy deer's eye. The deer, though dead, groaned and writhed in agony. A bookshelf to its left shifted, revealing a dark stairway leading downwards. The bookshelf held no books. In his mind, James scoffed; even with his reading difficulty, he had kept a few books with him in the years he had driven eighteen wheelers. Did the Qazanat promote anything healthy?

The slick stairway led to a room which held black crystal orbs, which Carl had used to show James Kala's memories. Memories she wouldn't have because Carl had forced them into her subconscious using his blood magic.

Vials of Kala's blood sat on the table next to where he would be chained. The guards forced him to chain himself then began to drip her blood onto the orbs. Their goal was obvious. He could sense the direction of their minds. They were trying to brainwash him; defeat his sense of self-worth, and eventually they would force him to fight his own daughter. What they hadn't seen in those memories was Kala's strength, her resilience, and her love of life.

But how much longer could he fight the compulsion? How much longer could Kala and Daniel withstand the tortures Carl tailored to their past traumas?

One of the Qurban entered, carrying a tray of syringes. "Hello, Selemati," James bowed towards him. "What does he have you doing today?"

"He tells me to inject you with the anti-spirit potion. You're to have no food, or water, for a week. He will kill me if you continue to resist him."

"He says that, but he needs you. No one else can do what you do."

"No." Selemati lowered his head. "He has captured my brother, Mordami. I try to resist Carl yet somehow I still harm my own blood, forcing Mordami to become like me." Selemati sighed. "How do you resist him?"

"I know who I am, what I believe in. I believe in God, and Kala, and Daniel." James smiled and sighed. "We have a bond stronger than Carl's hate and obsession. If you could resist Carl, what would you do?"

Selemati set the syringes down. "I would free my brother and the others Carl tortures. I would seek my family and reunite as many families as I could. I would create a cure for what I've created." He looked at the floor. A single, blood-filled tear trickled down his cheek.

"Keep that in your mind and heart."

Selemati smiled. "Thank you. I will do that. Still, I must inject this potion into you. The compulsion is too strong."

"Do what you must. Carl won't defeat me."

As the potion entered James' bloodstream, his sense of direction flickered. His muscles tightened and, as he breathed, he imagined the sea air and of seagulls calling his name. He thought of Kala's smile and his muscles relaxed.

Selemati started for the door, stopped, then looked back. "I will do what I can for Kala and Daniel. You have helped me today, dear friend. I will help them in return."

James smiled. "Thank you, Selemati. I have faith in you. Have faith in yourself, and you can fight the compulsion Carl's placed in you."

Selemati bowed his head towards James then left. Images formed on the black crystal orbs. James focused on the images, smiling as Kala fought against what she feared most. Pride filled him; she was stronger than she could ever know.

Kala woke in the Void, unaware of time, space, or reason, but she felt healthy, energized, and... pain free? How? Maybe she had done the right thing by ignoring her issues. That scared her. The last time she'd blocked her emotions, she had walked right into danger. In fact, that had happened this time too!

Dammit, Kala! You did it again!

She struggled to get free from herself, trying as hard as she might to get rid of all the filth. She felt she had earned this treatment. She was a whore and always would be one. No matter what, she would be in a situation like this.

NO!

She couldn't keep berating herself. There would be time enough for that later. Right now, she had to figure out where she was. The Void. She was suspended in a dark room and she couldn't feel the floor. Nor could she feel her muscles, bones, anything. It all felt like the weightless moment she had felt in her room back home. Was this like her protective shield? If so, why did Carl think it would be a punishment? Also, why hadn't the Qurban given her a potion? Carl seemed to expect obedience, as if he had had no problems before. Hmm… that was an avenue to explore later. She looked around in the darkness.

Though she saw or felt nothing, she could sense she floated above water. The slight whooshing sound of waves crashing, the trickle of a dainty waterfall, and a sound of thunder over the open sea filled her ears and mind. It was like a magical sound machine.

She made a mental note to teach herself, then she laughed and spoke to herself out loud. "Daniel always reminded me to do instead of say. Man, it's so lonely here. I need my friends, and since I don't have any real ones, any imaginary friend that wants to come back, will you join me?"

No one answered, which relieved her, but she didn't feel alone. She knew, somehow, that she would find a way out, a way to disappear and have the time she needed to plan how she would free the others.

She imagined how she felt that first night as a prisoner of war in her training. Before she had been taught any skills. The people she saw out there, even the Qurban, all seemed lower than low in their moods, and she could not stand to see such misery.

What were those lights that had come from her eye? What would they do? She could learn, over time. First, to clear her mind as she had so many times during meditations. Breathing in, out, in, out, she slowed her breath, imagining the inhalation brought in joy and life as the exhalation took out any impurities within her.

Tiny beams of silver-white light flowed from her eyes as she breathed, until the room lit up brighter than she had ever seen. It was the most beautiful room, full of peace and focus. Pearls of every color adorned the walls, melted together until smooth, swirling together like a painting created by pouring paint onto a surface. The floor was six inches or so below her. With another breath, she landed on her tiptoes. She felt lighter than she had in the air, weightless as a feather in front of a fan.

The glass floor led to a dais which held two mirrors, both silver-blue like the clouds in the sky. They rolled together and separately, forming two human-like forms; one could have matched Kala and the other could have matched Daniel, but she wrote this off as a hallucination. It was easy to want your partner to help, but she felt selfish even wanting Daniel's help in this situation.

Bringing her racing thoughts back to the present, she tried her best to focus. Nothing would work. Her brain swirled again, just as it had before, and she was tugged back to the entrance. The Qurban grabbed her and pulled her out as though she had been in a cave. She had had no chance to explore what she saw. "How long was I in there?"

"Overnight. You must come with us." Five Qurban had been sent. Was she that dangerous?

"It is time for breakfast. Make sure you eat; you will need your strength. Here, put this on." The lead Qurban handed her a white cotton dress. "How did you heal yourself?" he whispered in alarm, and they gathered around to look. "None of us can stop the Master, not even if all of us work together. He compels us. He will learn; he demands to see you every day. I am sorry we cannot do more. Yet, there is something I ask. Will you try to find a cure? If you can, we will help you get out, protect you as we can."

Kala smiled but stopped at a look from the lead Qurban. "A cure? That's what you need? I wanted to try anyway. I will accept your help. I will do what I can to release you from that heinous asshole. By the way, I'm not helping you just to get free. I'm helping you so I can be myself. Speaking of which… what happened to Daniel and… my father?"

"They are here. The Qazanat want all three of you."

"Why is this organization after us? And how did you resist his compulsion about the potion last night?"

The lead Qurban shook his head. "I do not know the answer to either question. Your father tried to learn their goals after escaping last year but didn't have enough time before he was captured again. As for the potion, none of us had the desire to do what he commanded us to do; in fact, we brought you to the Void because we knew you would be safer here than with him.

"Your presence strengthens us, more than James' presence ever had. You both have a way with people… as does Daniel, from what I've witnessed."

"I don't understand any of this." Kala's mind spun so fast, she had to lean toward the ground to stay upright. A knot formed in her stomach; she breathed into the knot and focused her mind on releasing the pain, which dimmed with each exhalation.

"We do not have time now, but you will learn. I see that in you already."

"Where is Daniel, and my father?"

"Daniel is in the research room, down in the second basement. James is in his final stages of brainwashing on the fourth floor, where the guards and the fully-'trained' Qurban reside. They forced him to watch what was done to you, highlighting every time the Master harmed you. Many perish after being treated so, but he does not deserve such a fate. Nor do you."

The lead Qurban looked around. "We cannot be seen talking to you this way after his order to stay quiet. I must attach a leash to you," he said in a quiet voice as he lowered his eyes.

The leash was cold; it drew the heat from her ankle, up through her body. Kala put the dress over her head and shivered. The cotton was the roughest she'd ever felt and, while it covered her private parts, it did not cover enough of the rest of her. A breeze flowed between her legs to drive the point home. She followed the Qurban, her stomach growling as the knot released.

Great, I'm trapped even more now. I shouldn't have tried to escape so soon. Now I'll never get out of here.

She remembered what the Qurban said, that James and Daniel were there. But the Qurban were the bad guys, right? No, Carl was. And this Qazanat group. Surely, he was too weak to be in charge; who planned this scheme against her family, and what was their end goal? Was she wrong to feel empathy for the Qurban or wrong not to trust them? Which was the right choice? Was there a right choice? Too many questions, not enough answers. She could think about them later.

Her father had seen her so weak. Her heart raced again, and her mind raced faster. The more she looked around, the more she saw and felt the heartache. Every sorrow grabbed at her heart and the weight of the emotions pulled her down. She tripped, chipping her toenails on the coral as she stubbed her toes every other step. She needed to help Daniel and James. As much as she hurt, she couldn't imagine what kind of torture they each had.

Then it hit her. "I healed?" The Qurban shushed her and nodded his head.

Kala imagined they had been walking half an hour to reach the dining area, up ramps and ladders that led to this hallway, which she assumed was on the second floor. Looking ahead, she saw rows of women and children, some chained and others not. She wondered why some were free, but just for a moment. Each of the unchained women stood when their names were called: *Holland, Strawa, Senavia,* and twelve others whose names Kala did not hear through her mental chatter. At first, she wondered why they were called, then she looked closer. Each of those women were pregnant. Anger burned within her and the chain on her ankle heated in response. "Did they get pregnant here?"

"Yes," the Qurban responded with a look that said she would learn more later. They led her to a table, and she sat next to a woman who showed signs of recently having been beaten to a pulp. Her face was so swollen, Kala could not see her eye color or the shape of her features. Her hair was the same color as Kala's, pulled back in an uncombed bun. The lead Qurban gestured at her, so Kala guessed she needed to talk to the woman.

The Qurban left, and human guards took over. Everyone was quiet, but their pain drove Kala mad. She began to twitch and shake, trying to remain quiet in a place where the noise in her head deafened her.

She looked at the woman next to her. "Hi, I'm Kala."
Everyone, even the guards, turned her way. The other woman
didn't look at Kala. Instead, she placed her hand on Kala's leg for
a second before putting it back on her lap.

One of the guards backhanded Kala.

"What is it with backhanding here?" she asked as she licked the
blood from her lips. The bitter tang of iron told her she wasn't
deficient. A small victory.

When she talked back, the women hung their heads, but she
could make out gasps in their widened eyes. The little girls locked
gazes with her, eyes shining as if she was a hero. The guard who'd
backhanded her grabbed her by the hair. Her legs buckled and she
fell to the floor as she was dragged away, led like an unruly dog on
a leash once she could stand. "The Master of Blood will be here to
set you straight, wench."

Kala laughed at "Master of Blood" and earned a kick to her
back, which sent her sprawling. She wasn't quick to anger at normal
times, but she had passed the limits of what she would accept. She
jumped back up and grabbed the chain tied to her. She wrenched
it from the guard's hand, turning it into a whip. Her first strike left
a gash on his cheek, right under his eye.

The wound gaped and blood poured, dripping from his chin.
He pulled a filthy handkerchief from his pocket and placed it on
his cheek, grimacing before glaring at Kala. She smiled in response.

The other three rushed in to help guard one, but she rear-
kicked the lead guard, who toppled into the other like dominoes.
She went to run toward what looked like a window, but it wasn't
even a window. It was a small hole at the top of the stairs. Beyond
it was a room.

An enormous energy surged toward her; she quivered in fear.
Images formed in her mind: torture; grieving widows, widowers,

mothers, fathers, and children; and war. She closed her eyes and breathed. Her body quivered, cold seeped into her bones as the chain tightened around her ankle. This room… did it hold the fears of the Universe? If so, she would never escape…

The injured guard grabbed her by the hair and pulled her back to him, his blood smearing on her dress and in her hair. He pressed himself against her and said, "I don't care what our Master tells us. There's only one way to tame a beast like you."

He bent her over and pushed her down on the floor. He tied her hands and feet together with her face down and rear up. They each took turns on her, not limiting themselves to one orifice.

The ripping sensation was familiar, so she made herself relax. She did not cry, and she did not fear the men. Disappearing behind her protective screen, she accepted this pain as her life, and she shivered. They had taken her world, her love, her family. She considered herself nothing more than a sex object. They couldn't hurt her more than she already hurt.

laughed at memories from when she'd done this when she was young. She had been a strange child.

Now wasn't the time to pretend to be a dog, though, so she tried to untangle herself in every other manner she could think of. Despite the extra room, she couldn't free herself.

There was nothing left but to hang there and wonder when she would be freed by the guards. Sleep still didn't come and her heart raced, thumping loud enough to hear it in her ear canal as blood rushed to her head. She hung in the dark with only her thoughts to entertain her. Instead of entertainment, she got torment. Every bad thing she had ever done or had been done against her rushed into her mind, a free-for-all against her sense of self. Could she really be a good person if this was her life?

She cried until snot flowed from her nose, her eyes puffed up, and her voice creaked when she sighed. After the tears stopped, she slept. Without her ring or her love, nightmares would be her only companions.

In her dream, Daniel stood right in front of her yet she could not reach him through the wavy, translucent veil that separated them. She couldn't hear her own voice or see her reflection in the mirror to the right of him, on her side of the veil.

The mirror in front of her looked like the one in the Void. Maybe this was a hint.

Gazing at Daniel, she had to make a choice. Would she obsess until she discovered how to reach him? Or would she look at the mirror which was clearer in her vision than he was? Her heart tugged her toward the mirror. Perhaps it would help her hone her magic. In her mind, she whispered to Daniel, *I'll return, I swear.*

He looked up like he could hear her. She held back the tears that would drown her if she let go.

She was unchained in her dream, free to walk about on the solid, forest-green marble floor. The trek to the mirror was easier than pie. Again, her thoughts raced. How was pie easy? The crust alone was a headache and a half. *Wait, focus. You can do it, Kala. It's a mirror, ask it questions.*

She reached out to touch the mirror. It turned into an ice cold, smooth liquid which began to morph into what looked like different versions of herself. One would be heavier with longer hair; one would be strong with a shaved head and fauxhawk. Others were smaller, thinner, like her childhood self. The last one she didn't fully recognize. It was taller, with more scars and bruises. Yet it was smiling a real smile, not the manic one she often had. The eyes were kind and hard at the same time. She cared about others but was beginning to identify more with this new version; she wasn't a doormat.

That's who Kala had wanted to be all along. How could she reach this state and be a human instead of a ball of everyone's emotions? She would find answers in this place, then she would go to Daniel to help him. She had a sense they would need to rescue James together.

She felt she had an idea of what was to come. Her gut told her she would survive this, and she trusted that feeling. She went back to stare at Daniel some more. His light brightened her, though the wavy veiled pane of glass between them distorted the glow. As she talked to his image through her mind, she felt at peace.

When she woke, she had no clue how long she had slept yet she felt refreshed and whole. A small part of her knew she was captive and everyone was in danger. She sat up and stretched, pulling the revealing dress down as she moved. She was still in the nightmare room yet she was freed from the pole and her chains.

She could see Daniel as she had in the dream, as if through a veil. He looked anguished. Something was wrong; he was in pain. She had to get to him. If she could heal herself this well, she knew she could do something. That's what magic was, right? Healing?

How did I pass out? God damn, I'm fucking weak.

Kala could hear an unidentified voice, speaking those words in her head, though she knew she had not passed out. So who was speaking in her mind? Daniel? Could they speak to one another through telepathy?

You're not weak, she said in her mind to the unidentified voice. *I felt the same drag, but it was familiar to me. I think that's how I stayed awake, though quite insane in my thought process.*

Kala? She could hear the voice in its entirety now. It was Daniel, weakened and afraid, though she could hear anger in his voice.

She felt the fear beneath the anger and became more afraid herself. *Daniel? Are you hurt?*

Yes, but not as much as others. I can't show the enemy what I show to you.

And neither can I. I'm scared, too. They have me in this black room where fearful energies reign supreme. There's another similar room, called the Void; it was peaceful instead of haunting. I think these rooms are meant to trap me inside my own head, but I've been trapped my whole life. I'm ready to escape.

Be patient. We will be better together than apart.

Daniel sounded nervous that she would walk into another mess. She couldn't guarantee she wouldn't either, which sent her mind into overdrive.

I will be patient. I have this sensation inside me in the Void, like a whirlwind climbing up from my arches to my brain, stopping just before it hits the energy center at the crown of my head. Then it spirals back down, to begin again. I'm bleeding everywhere but feel like I'm healing faster. What do you feel?

Pain of a thousand torches lighting inside me, burning me from the inside out. Each muscle contracts out of order, as if some clumsy pianist wants to create a "masterpiece". They created holes in my already herniated spine, but somehow I'm not reacting and it's pissing these bastards off. Triumphant music flowed to her from their bond.

I'm not reacting how the Qazanat want either. She growled. *Why did they target me like this? I'm so sorry for getting you into this!*

Kala, stop. This won't help. We will talk about why he targeted you when we get out. I need to sleep, and you need to ground. I love you. Please remember that.

Please remember the same from me. I love you, and they can't do anything to stop me from loving you.

Daniel was gone, and Kala breathed easier knowing he was at least alive. She needed to harness her powers. To find her powers, she needed to find her father.

"Daddy," she said aloud in the still darkness. "I need your guidance. And some information. When I was young, you told me what I needed to know to find my own way. Please, help me again."

She closed her eyes and breathed, feeling as if she was back home in Tennessee, slowly gliding down from the Fall Creek Falls Overlook down to the water below. She kept her arms crossed in front of her chest as she descended, rotating like a drill once she opened her eyes.

She took in the swirling as she had during youth rally games she had participated in. She remembered winning the "Dizzy Daisy" award for spinning the longest—ten minutes! Why she was proud

81

Kala sighed. "For years, I had the urge to call you. Once, when I had blacked out from all the stress, I called and asked to talk to you. Momma started crying and I couldn't handle it, so I just said I missed you and was drunk dialing. Now I know I sensed you. Why did you go to Daniel instead of me, especially after we broke up?"

"I was instructed to go to Daniel first, so he could prepare you for flight."

"Who told you this?"

"Naomi and Gul, some special people from this world." James' face reddened and he turned away.

"Is there something Momma needs to know?" Kala felt a little uneasy. Memories from her previous marriage resurfaced, but she saw them in a new light. Money had exchanged hands in her peripheral vision before her ex-husband had forced her into their bed with other men, sometimes two at a time. Her ex was a heavy-set man, almost a foot taller than her and four times her size in width. Her fear resurfaced and the peace dimmed. She gulped and quivered. Why had she just laid there, pretending to sleep, while the men touched her? Did she think they would respect her wishes to sleep? What stupidity! She was tired of being afraid.

"It's nothing like that," James said when he saw the disgust written on her face. He placed a warm hand on her shoulder, calming the tension.

"I'm not judging, Daddy. I just need to know... everything! I'm so tired of being confused..."

"Go back to the Void. Breathe, like you do naturally when at ease. The white light you used against Carl, use it again. Hone it. Practice with your blue fire as well. Build up physical strength, mental strength... Remember your POW training, not the traumas that distracted you from your goals. The answers will come when your mind is quiet."

He was right;, she already had the answers. She just needed to train more. "Yes, Daddy. I shall." After a kiss on the cheek for one another, and a bear hug that rivaled all others, Kala opened her eyes and was in the nightmare room.

Instead of turmoil, she felt peace. It was different from the peace she felt with Daniel. Daniel's peace was fire under the surface, raging with the heartfelt passion and obsession for his well-being. She tried to help everyone, so it made sense she would put her heart into the one she chose for life.

But she overdid it. All the time. Trying to save others when she needed to look out for herself. Why did she do it? Over and over she asked the question, "Why do I sacrifice myself?"

She breathed to quiet the raging storm. The image of Fall Creek Falls formed in her mind, but she focused on what was below the surface. The stone platform did not waver, though such a powerful source would erode it over time. Neither the pounding water, nor the stone would be more powerful than the other—each would have their pros and cons. Her thoughts rode the waterfall as it journeyed, pounding on the rocks and becoming still after the initial upset of impact.

The pain she had ignored filled her to the brim. Her heart felt like it had been ripped apart, freeze-dried, and shattered into shards that would pierce her skin if she picked up the pieces. Lacerations inside her ripped apart and she became weak, head flopping as she tried and failed to correct her posture.

Each time she worried about an issue, another would arise. Alternating points throughout her body writhed as though electrocuted, causing Kala to writhe in turn. She breathed through it all, determined to heal herself instead of wallowing. Wallowing helped no one.

She pulled herself up and ran toward the mirror. Only lumps of silver remained, but light spilled from them, a light that replaced the shadows within her. She searched for a way out and found none. When she rushed to where she had been held, she saw blood on the floor. As she reached the puddle of congealed blood, it returned to liquid and surged towards her with the speed of a violent wave.

She did not avoid it, she stood tall. It flooded over her, staining her hair and the dress, neither of which she cared about. Somehow, her face remained unbloodied and her mind was at peace.

The blood disappeared only to be replaced with tortured people: men, women, children, and animals ripped apart in front of her eyes. Daniel and James weren't there, but it didn't make a difference. Everyone needed help. She breathed deep and imagined the blue fire within her consuming the bad guys. One by one, they caught fire, melting in the heat of her flames, their shrill screams echoed through the room. The people escaped with tears and widened eyes which shone in the blaze as they glanced back at their attackers. No one seemed to see her, and when she called out to them to be careful, not one of them responded.

It all seemed real. Was she invisible? No, it made sense that the people would be too scared to hear her through the roar of the flames or the screams of their attackers.

This wasn't the Void; she could feel the difference in the energies—the fear remained, yet in her dreams she had been at peace. How did this room work? Since she could burn the bad guys to a crisp, could she learn to control this room and the Void? Lost in thought, she didn't see the guard approach. He punched her in the stomach; the pain forced her to bend over. He uppercut her in the face and she grunted as the pain gripped her.

Vomit spewed from her mouth onto the ground, growing into vines which surrounded them, leaving her no way to escape. He forced shackles on her wrists then beat her until she felt her blood pressure rise to heal the injuries. Then every blow bounced off her, leaving her with only minor rib injuries. "You're coming with us," he said, half-dragging her out of the room.

Kala said nothing; she focused her energy on finding Daniel. Was he in this place, or was it a ruse? She felt his light as well as his pain. He was somewhere in Terois Manor. She wasn't being led to him; she would find a way to him on her own. She would free him from whatever pain was inflicted upon him, just as she healed herself.

The guards led Kala up to the fifth floor, down the same corridor as before. Carl's. Kala gritted her teeth and considered her options. He would get his comeuppance one day. She just had to be patient. And calm. They would not win if she remained calm. She could play the defeated warrior well.

When the guards pushed her into the room, she pulled her shoulders back and down, lengthened her spine, and focused on a point beyond Carl's head. She would get through whatever was issued to her; she took comfort from this. Nothing could break the spirit of a wolf or an owl. She would maintain her spirit and grow stronger.

Carl sneered at her. "You think you're strong? Ha! You're nothing but a whore for my pleasure, and you will learn that. Bend over."

Kala said nothing. She continued to stare straight forward, ignoring the slimy foe as though he were nothing. He grabbed her chin, forcing her towards his, and commanded her to kiss him. She kneed him in the groin instead. Power surged through her and she smiled.

Fury twisted his features and he slapped her then forced her onto the bed and ripped off the dress that covered one-third of her body. "A whore needs no clothes." He snarled as he violated her with claws and hammers, pounding a piece of wood that barely fit into her while one of the Qurban held her down for him.

She told herself she was somewhere else and attempted to ignore her feelings. She looked into the sad eyes of the Qurban; she felt he wanted to let her go.

Wincing, she stared longer into the Qurban's eyes to give him strength to fight Carl's control. The ring Carl wore pressed inside her as though it was trying to become one with her body, and the Qurban gripped her harder despite the emotions in his eyes. She felt every agonizing movement, but she escaped into her mind, just as she would escape Terois Manor at some point. She had to have hope, to survive. In that moment, she knew she would have to kill him to escape.

While he eviscerated her, she contemplated whether she could kill another man. She had never wanted to; she had only wanted to heal people. But she had learned through military training when the use of force, even lethal force, was necessary. The Qazanat went out of their way to destroy people's lives. If killing was necessary, so be it. She hoped they might come back one day with a pure soul. It was strange for her to be this calm about such a violent topic.

She could not hold on to herself anymore. Each jolt of pain became the only thing she could focus on; her feeble struggles did nothing to stop the onslaught. She couldn't keep fighting. She wanted to die. But every time she began to pass out, Carl slapped her in the face, bloodying her lip further, refusing to give her any peace. She wondered what the point of this was, or if there was any point other than torture for the sake of torture. How could anyone get off at another's pain? This had to be the definition of evil.

When Carl was done with her, he threw her off the bed. "Throw this dress in the garbage. She won't need it. As I said before, a whore needs no clothes."

The Qurban led her stumbling back to the Void, where they had some space away from other guards.

They made their way in silence, half-carrying Kala until she demanded they let her walk on her own. She refused to show her weakness, refused to limp though her entire body spasmed, bringing tears to her eyes. She sniffled and swallowed the phlegm, groaning at how disgusting it felt.

"Why isn't this room guarded like the others?" she blurted as they arrived at the Void, which she guessed was on the ground floor, though it was hard to tell—Terois Manor was a gigantic maze that made her brain swirl if she focused too hard.

The Qurban looked around, making sure no one else could hear, then said, "No one knows how this room works. They believe it is just a Void, a black space where one could float for eternity. But I know different.

"The Abeja legend of Terois Manor says that the Roshanra healer will discover its secrets and free the people from tyranny. I believe that is you, for you are the only one who has tolerated a night in the Void, healing yourself in the process. The Qazanat do not seem to know about this, or maybe Carl is operating outside their knowledge? Either way, the Qurban all feel drawn to you. We want to keep you safe. Yet we cannot."

"What would free you? Is there anything I can do from in here?" Kala looked around, focusing both on the Qurban and the building. When she breathed in, she heard screaming throughout

Terois Manor. All this screaming was nothing compared to the fear she felt, both her own and these others. Hatred, disgust, even love poured from the people and was absorbed into her as she stood there. She was vulnerable; she could not block all the sensations. Everything swirled behind her eyes and she almost lost her balance.

"First, you must heal. Carl has compelled us to bring you to him for the next twelve days. For more and more torture each time. Can you make it through that?"

"I don't know, but I can sure try. Oh, I noticed you didn't refer to him as your master this time."

The Qurban's mouth hung open in surprise, then he smiled. His teeth seemed white underneath the yellow-green scales which were forming over them. "You are correct! I think you are helping us already."

"What are your names?"

"I am Leopold Terois, the owner of Terois Manor. My wife, Caroll, was taken away to be a... whore... in another realm. We cannot call them anything else. This is Casey Storm, the prince of Abeja." Leopold looked both sad and angry, and Kala had no doubt as to his honesty.

Casey bowed his head as he was introduced and gave a sad smile. "It pleases me to meet such a powerful ally, but I fear it is not enough. Even now, all our allies are split up, and I do not know where to find them. Rumor says my sister lies below, but I am forbidden to search the manor."

Kala said nothing and bowed her head in return, acknowledging his statement. She didn't understand why everyone had taken an interest in her, nor did she believe she was a powerful ally. They could be looking for any sign of weakness to report back to Carl. Questions formed in her mind.

"Is there a library here with information on the... Roshanra, you say?"

"Yes, there is," Leopold replied, smiling with pride in his eyes. "The library encompasses the entire third floor; we are forbidden to go inside."

"Does Carl track all your movements?"

Casey looked at Kala with wide eyes. "I have never thought of it that way. I do not know where his power comes from, but it blocks my sense of self. It has worked that way with everyone else, even the women who are used as breeding mares; the Qurban mutation only works on men. Perhaps the way you and your kin treat us is what gives us strength." Casey bowed his head with a smile.

Leopold took Kala's hand and led her to the edge of the Void before whispering, soft enough that she strained her ears to hear, "You hold the keys to healing in your heart. Master the Void to keep those keys."

"What..."

But Leopold turned away. "Sleep well, miss." He shut the door to the Void.

Kala stepped back and found herself floating again. She wondered over his statement, not knowing how to master something she hadn't trained in. She had read stories containing riddles, yet she had never thought she would be forced to solve one herself.

Pain kept her from thinking, kept pulling her further and further into the past, and she had trouble thinking of anything else.

What had Carl done to her? She remembered tools being used, something pinching inside her, and the wetness soaking into the bed he had used. Not knowing why she was there or why she was tortured increased the anger inside her. She clenched her fists, determined to find a way out, to safety. Then she would find a way to get *everyone* out, not just those she loved.

She was committed, she wouldn't be stopped without a fight. Closing her eyes, she took several slow, deep breaths, lengthening more each time, just as she had practiced in therapy. Now she saw the value of mindfulness; she didn't think she would have fared as well otherwise. As Kala breathed, she lowered herself into the area she had found before.

Once she landed on the ground, she found herself looking up. A clear ceiling separated her from the swirling darkness. Strange... the darkness had seemed so still.

A chill ran through her and brought goosebumps to her arms and legs. *Goosebumps armor,* Kala thought and laughed. An image of her in pimply skin-toned armor gave her a diseased impression. In fact, that was what the Qurbans' greying skin looked like—lizard armor.

It was the same room as before yet the scenery had changed. The pearls were darker, like someone had painted them, leaving spots of light pinks and cream colors which were there before. The mirrors ahead looked different as well. They did not morph or move or do anything out of the ordinary. They sat there, beckoning for Kala to investigate.

As Kala moved toward the mirrors, she felt more aches and pains. She was back in that torture room, yet she knew it was a flashback. She was used to those, could see past them to the present. And, in the present, a lake formed between the mirror and herself, pushing the mirror further away. She could either swim or find a way across.

Swimming was always wonderful for Kala's mind, yet she knew nothing about the lakes here. They could be acidic, have predators that would smell the blood still leaking from her wounds, any number of things. She circled the lake until she came to a raft created from small planks of wood.

She wasn't familiar with rafting yet she knew how to row. There was a short paddle, one she would have to use while squatting low and duck walking to the other side. She could see a bridge across the way, one that started in the middle of the lake.

She pushed the raft into the water and climbed onto it, careful not to tip it in the process. The raft had seemed larger before she climbed on. She had no room to move around, and no sail assisted her travels. Sitting in the middle, she used the paddle to row her way to the bridge.

Soon her arms tired, so she had to take a short break, but the tide began to push her back so she had to paddle again. Left and right she rowed, attempting to travel in the right direction. She felt the raft become smaller, as though it was melting into the water. Soon there would be no more raft.

She had to make a choice. If she jumped off the raft, she would have to swim. At the thought, her arms screamed for mercy, but she let it pass. The other choice was to stay on the raft until it melted away; she would need time to adjust her position in the water. She recalled falling into a pool that way once, and she had bobbed around like a buoy on a lake. Her mind was set, she would jump in.

It was awkward getting to a standing position. The raft had shrunk and would split apart if a goldfish bumped into it. Without another thought, she took a breath and jumped in, holding her nose in the process.

The water jolted her brain, it felt like ice. Goosebumps raised over her arms and legs and her nose stung. She thought she would not make it, but she pushed the thought aside. She had to make it, not just for her sake but for the sake of all the captives. As she

Sonaria smiled. "The Void is the power that comes from compassion, a power you have possessed since your birth. During battle, it protects spirit walkers, like you. Those who are loved by the spirit walker also have the protection and potential to spirit walk with him or her."

Kala furrowed her brow. "Spirit walker? I thought I was an Empath Healer. How can I be both?"

Sonaria laughed, a twinkle in her eye. Her lava hair glowed brighter. "Have you ever had what's called an 'out of body experience'?"

"Sometimes for years on end."

"That is a form of spirit walking. The soul wants to remain pure, especially in those with a lot of heart. Your spirit escaped what you could not, so you could harness your power when the time was right."

"So I hone that skill to get free?"

"Hone all your skills to save the worlds."

Kala marveled at the woman who was smaller yet stronger in so many ways than Kala could ever be. Why didn't her lava hair burn her?

Then it hit her; others sacrificed for her. Nausea welled. She wanted to scream.

Sonaria laughed.

"Why are you laughing?" Kala remembered she was naked; she crossed her arms to cover her breasts. It would look like she had to pee if she covered her nether regions, so she avoided it.

"I can hear your thoughts. Like you, I am an Empath. I'm here to help you begin your destiny of Empath Warrior. You will be one of the strongest who has ever lived. But you must be kept secret until you have mastered your training. Two others, your kindred, must receive different training. Your task whilst you are here will be to deliver my message to them and to learn as much as you can on your own."

"I assume you mean Daddy and Daniel, the ones who came with me?"

"Yes. They will have their own tasks, but you must transmit a secret message to them both." Sonaria handed a dagger to Kala; it was made of pure sapphire with a silver handle. She had never seen a blade made of sapphire but could sense it was powerful in many ways. "This is yours, to use in your most desperate moments. Do not carry it with you. Hide it in the Void so you may call on it when you need to, no matter where you are."

Energy surged through Kala's hand, and into her body. When she closed her eyes, the energy overtook her, and she could hear Sonaria's thoughts in her mind. *Free the people, all of them, help them learn and evolve. For immortals drive the Qazanat and seek to destroy us all.*

7

When Kala opened her eyes, she was back at the beginning of the Void. The darkness pushed in, yet she was at peace. The dagger was gone but she could see it in her mind's eye. It shone bright and gave her strength for what lay ahead. Torture, more and more each day, being used however Carl, the Master of Blood, saw fit. But that didn't scare her. She knew in her gut she would survive.

She needed sleep, but she couldn't. Instead, she felt manic. Her arms felt sore from rowing and swimming, her whole body was taut from the effort. Yet she felt calm in the face of these struggles.

Her goal was clear; she had to contact her father and Daniel. And no one could know, not even the Qurban. Trust didn't come easy for her, after all she had been through. She closed her eyes and was pulled back out of the Void by the chain she had forgotten was still attached to her ankle.

As soon as she left the Void, a fist landed across her cheek. She did not wince, though the pain radiated through her body—her brain seemed to block anything unpleasant. It was the guard from the previous day. This time, she would not let him get her riled up. She would give them no excuse to predict her actions.

Nor would she show how hurt she was, how much she wanted to escape, and her goals to protect others. That was the hard part, because in that moment she saw children walk past, bruised and bleeding, their faces despairing. She would find a way to give them comfort or she would die trying.

The guard noticed she was unfocused and kicked her in the ribs a few times. Each kick made breathing a torture. As the guard led her to the feeding area, which was larger than she thought, she stumbled a little.

Hundreds of women and little girls, even some little boys, sat naked with their heads down, eating only when the guards looked toward them.

"Eat fast or you will regret it," the guard ordered before he left her tied to the bench.

She knew she couldn't speak at mealtimes, but she wanted to contact the woman next to her. She saw a resemblance in their facial features and a similar aching in their spirits.

The woman noticed her and shook her head enough for Kala to see, telling her not to speak. She slipped something under the table to Kala, who had nowhere to hide anything.

When she took it, the item wriggled inside her wrist like a parasite. It tickled more than it hurt. She had the feeling it was hiding, so Kala just let it be.

Everyone got the same meal. Grey mush and more white mush. For some it might have been flavorless, but Kala had always tasted the undertones in her meals. She was known in nutrition science classes as a super taster. This meal had something unseemly in it, but she could not tell what it was. Without thinking, she put her hand over the food and thought of it as clean and nutrient-rich,

Carl's children? She closed her eyes and breathed through the pain. In her mind, she focused on her womb, bringing up a pregnancy prevention shield.

This wasn't the first time she had been beaten, and she was certain it wouldn't be the last.

After he was done, he spat at her before he called in his Qurban, Leopold Terois himself. It made sense; the head honcho would take on the most important role.

Leopold's bright green eyes looked at her before he looked at his master, which earned him a slap as well. He looked like he wanted to growl but straightened his face and bowed to Carl as though he accepted his life with ease.

"Chain her up then leave her there until I return. I have to retrieve an item." Carl was out the door without a word to Kala, leaving her bleeding on the floor.

"I am sorry, I must do as he says." Leopold looked away from Kala's naked body while he tied her to a hanging bar which was suspended over the bed. The cord glowed blood red and seemed to seep into her skin and coagulate. She wondered if she would be able to loosen it but Leopold answered her unspoken question with, "Only the Master can release this bond." He left her chained, bruised, and bleeding... again. When would it end?

After what seemed like hours, Carl returned with a contraption that looked like a whisk with sandpaper for edges and a whip. Kala did not have to ask to know why he retrieved them. He loved to cause pain, the bloodier the better.

Dread filled her and her vision swam. She didn't faint, but her mind went to another place while he tortured her, put the whisk inside her, and whipped her, a place that felt like the Void. Was her protective screen the Void all along? She stayed within the Void in her mind while he used her for his physical pleasures, not bothering to clean up his mess afterward.

He pushed a button and a box appeared next to him.

It was black, approximately four-by-four feet. Even before he released her shackles, she knew he would put her into the box. She didn't mind this part; the darkness would be better than seeing his face.

He forced her inside and closed the door, leaving her to her own thoughts, which became darker by the moment. In the darkness, she still saw his face.

Now she was miserable, she could not recall the times of happiness, every inch of her body rioted against her. She could feel her blood on the floor beneath her, her insides felt as if they had been ground to a pulp. She wanted the pain to stop.

How could she ever feel happy again? She was a puppet, meant to be destroyed, used for entertainment.

She fell asleep soon after, crammed into the tiny space. Kala's body tingled as numbness approached, and she withdrew into herself. Her dreams were the only things that would keep her sane.

* ☾ ☼ *

Kala's dream began with a tulip blooming in front of her. Rain, snow, and wind tried to beat it down. The tulip refused to budge, refused to die—it was a miracle of nature. It picked itself and floated in the air to Kala, as if a gentle hand grasped it. When she took it, her spine straightened like the flower's strong stem, refusing to give itself over to the storm. Muscles toned and fat disappeared, leaving her feeling as if she could tackle the world and tickle it to happiness. She smiled.

8

Daniel woke to water dripping on his head. The room was dark, dank, and gave him a headache. His muscles tightened where he was chained to the floor by a cable he could neither see, move, nor break. His hands were tied tight to his ankles, his knees ached and begged to straighten. The cable wrapped him, up and down his body.

He tried to roll over, but to no avail. His butt prickled from lack of circulation; so did his hands, his feet, most of his body. He was one giant nerve ready to snap as soon as he was free.

He had had plenty of time to think, but no helpful thoughts came. He worried about Kala, worried about James, and worried about himself. He tried not to think like a victim, but he had been kidnapped and tortured, how could he not be a victim? James had told him about these creatures, but Daniel could not believe so many people had been changed into mutants. At least twenty had captured them, and there were many more in this location. More than one hundred people could fit in the dungeon. He estimated that three quarters of their captors were Qurban.

A door opened in front of him; the light blinded him. He turned his head to dim the blindness but still looked to see a shadow standing in the doorway. A man walked through and bent down with a knife. Scorching fuels of hatred and fear combined as the knife neared him. There was nothing he could do; he would die if that was the man's plan. The invisible chains released instead. The knife had not cut but poked, like a button needed to be found.

"Come," the man said. He was a shell of a man, which wrenched Daniel's heart—he had felt like that before. The man was dressed as a guard but his puke green uniform was loose and rumpled. His eyes were flat, no light was reflected from them, and his brown hair looked like it was half-combed, half-pulled-out.

"Where are we going?" Daniel kept the emotion he felt from his voice.

"To see the doctor," he said with an accent like the Dari linguists Daniel had worked with. "He will assess you, then relocate you."

He guessed this man knew nothing of the assessments, so he asked instead, "What's your name?"

The man looked at him and blinked slowly, as if trying to overcome surprise. Had no one cared to ask his name before? "My name is Nedrick Slimbers, sir."

"Nice to meet you, Nedrick. I'm Daniel Blood." Daniel offered his hand which Nedrick took with his mouth open in amazement.

Music played in Daniel's head and he sighed. His sigh echoed through the room and the same music began to play in the hall. The sewer-like structure allowed it to echo further, growing like an orchestra in an opera house. The acoustics in this dungeon were fantastic.

"What are you?" Nedrick said, still not releasing Daniel's hand.

"I'm just a man learning new tricks." He pulled his hand free and said with a braver face, "Lead me to this doctor."

Nedrick led Daniel through the dungeon. The walls were made of cycling water through glass-like tiles. A stream flowed underneath his feet, leaking through the glass floor. Terois Manor itself seemed tortured. Every twist and turn disoriented Daniel—he'd never be able to find his way back on his own.

He tried to remember when and where he turned, but the turns could all have been the same. Sometimes it seemed they walked through walls of water, which didn't surprise him in this magical world compared to his logical one.

The cold seeped into him, yet he did not mind. He had grown up in the snow and ice and, with the right means, he knew how to stay warm and dry. But he probably wouldn't have blankets or heaters or any other comfort items; the Geneva Conventions didn't exist for evil corporations. Someone had to figure out a way to defeat them.

After ages of walking on tingling legs, he entered what could have been a normal doctor's office. Nedrick told him to wait there, then left with a slight hesitation. Daniel's mind raced with scenarios of what could happen in this room.

A metal table sat in the middle of the room; this wasn't a normal hospital. Hand and foot straps were bolted to the sides. He moved closer. The straps were stained and worn; his mind filled with an image of people straining until they bled. The tools in the office were an assortment of syringes, bandages, and torturous-looking tools. The least menacing tool was a set of pliers, which he assumed took out splinters and fingernails. He shivered at the thought, glad he never had to do that to anyone. Maybe he could steal a scalpel.

As he moved towards the tools, the door opened without a knock. A Qurban in a lab coat walked in, eyes shining green with curiosity. Daniel looked around again—there was no window to escape.

The Qurban reached out his hand and Daniel obliged, giving him his own. No music this time, but he could feel the man's pulse, slower than his own.

Daniel waited for the Qurban to speak. "I will be your doctor during your stay." There was a slight waver in his voice, like he wasn't sure of himself and what he was doing.

He asked Daniel to strip off his clothes and lie down, noting each scar and tattoo—he paused at the horned monster tattoo with dozens of rows of teeth—then pushed Daniel back to a sitting position on the table. The cold metal was a shock on his skin. It shouldn't have been that cold.

Later, Daniel sat in a cell in the dungeon of the mysterious building. Only the Qurban came to talk to him, and each had a deference he did not expect. They tortured him and apologized for torturing. Every time they did, he wanted to punch them right between the nose, show them he did not accept their apologies.

Where was Kala? Why had she left? There had to be a reason; her normal self was codependent. Well, he had to give her a hand for being able to separate from him, but she had chosen the worst time to do so!

Every time he mused, the shock waves started again. His body tried to curl into a ball, but screws in his shoulders and spine kept him where he was. His arms, legs, and neck could move, so he guessed they hadn't messed with his spinal column. But it sure felt

The man introduced himself as Carl Arresto, the "Master of Blood", which made Daniel laugh.

"You're not my master," Daniel said. He saw confusion on Carl's face and held back a smile.

"Master, his surname is Blood," Selemati said when Carl looked at him for clarification. Selemati must have overheard Daniel's conversation with Mordami.

"Lift him," Carl demanded.

Selemati pressed a button on a remote control, and the bolts lifted Daniel off the floor so his feet hung down.

"For his insolence, he will remain like this until I say otherwise. Even at night. Draw his blood in other ways." Carl smiled; blackened shadows discolored the enamel, his gums bulged, outlined in red.

"Where's Kala?" Daniel tried to ignore the burning nerves in his spine. He had to work hard to avoid gritting his teeth.

"Oh, you're the one she spoke of. She's mine; you will die before you get her back. Thanks for making her fresh meat again." With a malicious laugh, Carl left; he looked as if he had won.

Daniel smiled; Kala wouldn't break. Neither would he.

Selemati followed Carl, and Daniel heard a slap before he returned.

"What happened?" Mordami asked Selemati, who held his cheek and glared at the floor.

"He hit me because this one is not changing." Selemati pointed at Daniel but smiled at him when he said it. "It must be true; you are one of the Foreseen. Is this Kala another?"

"Yes," Mordami said. "Kala is the spawn of James." Murmurs began along the wall. "The Roshanra are all here, it would seem. Escape is inevitable." Mordami looked at the others. "It will get worse before it gets better, but you will see, the Foreseer's puzzles cannot lie."

Daniel thought about what Mordami had said; it confirmed what James had told him. They were all central to some plot. What could that plot be? Kala had visited his dreams; he knew they were real, just as he knew their telepathic connection was real. But he hadn't tried to reach out to her since. He hadn't protected her; how could he help her now?

Kala had indicated she was raped daily, by multiple men. Why would the Qazanat mutate and rape the Roshanra, other than to control them? What set them apart from the people of Derowa?

He only knew what James had taught him, things like concealing powers and navigating the land. James had also done something to Daniel's mind when he placed his hand on Daniel's shoulder. It was welcomed and approved, but Daniel couldn't understand yet what James had done. How long until the magic affected his brain?

Hanging by the bolts was excruciating at first until his lower body and arms stretched. His muscles loosened but his spine radiated pain every time he thought of something positive. Zap, zap... he could hear the sound in his mind, taunting him, urging him to think only of the pain. Too bad for the Qazanat; Daniel was used to pain.

He had a better view of the room from up here and could see out of the small window. There was no activity, and he could see a gate in the distance. He supposed they could make it out if no guards hung around that area. But where would they go?

Either way, James was in the final stages of becoming a Qurban, which Mordami had said was five years. That would mean Kala, James, and Daniel had been there almost a year, yet he would not give up hope. The problem was the Qazanat wouldn't give up either.

One day, Selemati came in with an extra bag of vials.

Mordami whistled, calling his brother over. "What are those for?"

Selemati looked at the floor and said, "The Master has ordered ten times the medication for Daniel Blood. He is determined you will be his, just like your woman and her father." He wiped his eyes and said with a sniffle, "He ordered me to tell you he keeps her in a cage and her father waits on them, with the Lord of the Manor."

Heat suffused Daniel's face; he screamed with rage. His muscles tightened and he ripped himself from his shackles. Blood and skin fragments spattered the wall.

"Where are they?" he growled.

Selemati smiled instead of looking afraid. "You are a marvel, sir. I am sorry to have done all this. I will help you." He released all of the cellmates and said, "The mutations make us stronger. That will work in our favor."

"How do I get to her?"

"You cannot go to her now. You must take a detour; it is written. She will find you." He looked at Mordami and smiled again. "I have done research in the library at night. There is a space under the Void, where the Foreseen must travel. Follow me; we must go now, before the Master learns of your escape."

To the others, Selemati said, "You will escape, and I will go with you. Somehow, his hold on us all is lessening. I will not harm you again."

Selemati turned to Mordami. "Do you recall the tree Gul planted nearby?" Mordami smiled and nodded. "Wait for me there. I will come without delay."

They all walked fast yet careful to tread quietly. Selemati led, followed by Daniel. The others turned right as they left the room and Mordami put a hand on Daniel's shoulder. His look said, "Good luck."

Daniel hesitated then followed Selemati to the left. He wanted to rush to Kala yet his instincts told him he needed to know more before he could match the Qazanat leaders. They had goons, he only had himself.

Kala would survive. She had said in their joint dream, even if the Qazanat wanted her dead, she would not rest until she was free. He could recall the clarity of her voice and the sincerity in her eyes. She looked beautiful, though bruised, bloody, and shaken. In his dreams, she did not talk about what happened; she would have in real life. She tended to over-share.

It wasn't the right time to muse; he snapped back to reality. He would learn all he could. Innocent lives were at stake. He couldn't do it alone, but he hoped he could save Kala and James so they could save the people together. If that was his path, his destiny, he would put his all into it. He would not give up, even if he died. *No, I can't die. They need me. She needs me.*

The hallway was long and dark, but he did not feel he had missed much while he had been thinking. Selemati was a cautious man, looking back and forth to ensure no one was coming. What would he say if he was caught?

They stopped, looked both ways, and waited without a word. Still, no one came.

Selemati reached his hand toward the wall of swirling water, pushed a block open and whispered, "Crawl through there and you will find the underside. I do not know what you must do, but the research I read in the library insinuates it is here. Rumors say your female made it below. I must go." He smiled and lay a hand on Daniel's arm. "Good tidings. Win for us all."

Daniel thanked him and watched as Selemati snuck back, heading to meet his brother and the others. He could not stay to watch. The sooner he got to the underside, the sooner Kala would be safe.

The block swung closed as Daniel crawled through the tunnel. His wounds stretched with each movement; he gritted his teeth to avoid screaming and forced his focus back to his task. The place could be booby trapped. If it was, he would be dead. Nonetheless, he continued to crawl through a space no bigger than one of the air conditioning ducts he had seen in movies.

The floor seemed to be made of coral and poked his knees and hands as he crawled. He was glad to have clothes and boots, even though he had not changed them in a while. James had told him the women didn't have that luxury.

After twenty minutes or so, he came to a brightly lit room. The tunnel had been dark; he shielded his eyes as he stood. After being in the cramped tunnel, his back spasmed and he crashed back down.

He stayed on the ground, breathing deeply through his nose. Gritting his teeth, he held his breath, exhaled long and slow.

"Daniel."

He jumped. He hadn't seen the woman approach, his back flared again.

"Come, sit with me a moment."

Daniel remained silent, curious rather than suspicious. She looked like a woman from one of his Kala dreams—her lava hair gave her away. She and Kala had been speaking as though he was not there. In the dream Kala was drenched, which he had attributed to this being a water building.

"I am Sonaria. You can see and talk to me because of Kala; your bond is stronger than I could have fathomed. You dream of each other. You sleep with one another each night while you are tortured during the day. Do you wish to be with her again?"

"Of course." How could Sonaria question his loyalty? Who was she to Kala?

"I ask because I must ask as much of you as I have asked of her. I have no ability to train her, but I gave her a tool before I sent her back to the hyenas. You are my trainee and must listen to my every command."

"First, tell me why you can't train Kala."

Sonaria hesitated. Her quick inhalation told Daniel she was nervous about something. "She is not whole. I can only train one who knows who they are."

Daniel knew she was correct. He hoped Carl and the Qazanat would not find out Kala's weakness as quickly.

She smiled. "So, we begin."

9

Kala was flung face-first into the cell. Even after weeks of torture, she could sense it was a different cell. This dungeon was not just damp, but dark and already inhabited by another woman.

Kala's feet splashed in water, and once or twice she sat down in it, patting at the surface with her hands and feet. She lay on her front and pretended to swim, and then to be eaten by a shark, then laughed at her own silliness. She had to do something to stay sane, after all.

"You will catch your death if you keep playing in the water," her roommate said. "You are not invincible."

"Well, what else is there to do?" Kala asked with as little sarcasm as she could. "We are stuck here, and we have to stay in the right mind to escape."

"No one has ever escaped Terois Manor. I do not see how we will start now." The woman approached from the shadows. Kala could feel the woman's curiosity, and the hopelessness that consumed them all. The air felt heavier on her lungs each day. She still didn't know where she was in relation to her own home. She assumed the portal had taken her to another world, maybe another universe. Before they were captured, James had called it Derowa, and she had never witnessed so much strangeness. At least the type of strangeness that others could also see.

"I forgot to ask your name," Kala said, still preoccupied with splashing, but not willing to stop—she knew that if she did her memories would surge again.

"I am Grace Storm, Princess of Abeja." She stepped into what little light existed in the dungeon. It was the first time Kala had seen her in the light, other than at the breakfast table. She stood tall, and her wounds were gone.

Kala stood too and walked closer, holding her hand out to shake Grace Storm's. It felt awkward not feeling anxious around a person. "I met your brother, Casey. He wanted me to look for you; I guess I found you."

"Casey is here?" Grace sat down with a splash, her eyes squinting, her brow creased with fear. "That means he has been turned into a Qurban. How else could they keep him away?"

Kala nodded and lowered her head.

"We may have a means to escape. What powers do you have? I can tell you are an outsider; rumor says you are one of the Foreseen. What can you do?"

"I can heal myself and sense emotions. Sometimes I think I can sense intent. White lights spill from me, but I'm not certain what they do, and I can emit blue fire as a shield. I think Carl affects my memory... I can't recall using the powers, but I see them in my mind's eye."

Kala's hands fidgeted, nails fighting one another to see which would chip first, another distraction technique—one that would

"It looks solid." She bent her fingers to grip the top. Her fingers went through the water.

"It is solid to most. It seems you are something of a traveler between worlds. Hone that and you can find a man everyone speaks of, he is called Daniel. He has resisted the mutation. If you find him, bring him here; I can hide him, and he will be comfortable... more comfortable than he is right now, I am guessing."

"How do you know all this?" Kala felt a sense of foreboding— what if she would never learn these tricks? She needed to find Daniel soon.

"As a water sorceress in a water cell, sound travels to me when I need it. As of now, I have only penetrated the dungeon areas; the laboratory is just down the hall. Perhaps this is the time to form a resistance. The Qazanat think they are invincible. We will show them they are not."

"I like your style. I can see you will be a formidable queen one day." Kala paused then said, "I think I need to meditate for a while. That is how I have honed my skills thus far, and they are not that honed. Mind training is what I need. And possibly heart training, because it will break my heart if anything happens to Daniel, or Daddy." With a look from Grace, she added, "Daddy was turned into a Qurban, and I think it was because of me."

"You may be right." Grace pulled her knees to her chest, just like Kala had done in the past when she needed protection. "The Qazanat thought I was you. That is why they attacked Abeja first. I am the reason my brother and parents were taken. The Qazanat have held me here until they could find the real Foreseen. I do not know what will happen to me now, or to my family."

"I won't let anything happen to you, if I can control it." Kala was resolute. She could do this; she had mastered survival techniques before. Now it was time not just to survive but to fight back.

Kala sat on her own bed. It was placed on a stone that jutted out of the walls at waist height. Kala hopped onto the bed, water dripping from her feet, drenching her thin, holey blanket.

The mattress was hard and lumpy, as if it had never been changed. The new master of this castle seemed determined there would be no peace in the land. One thing she knew, Carl wasn't following the Geneva Conventions.

She lay down on her bed, her feet flat and knees bent. It was her best position for meditation; she had a hard time staying awake when she had her knees down.

She slowed her breathing—deep breath in, deep breath out, sometimes a slight hold in the middle. Feeling the oxygen travel through her body and into her brain made her yawn. She didn't mind those yawns; they stretched her tense jaw, loosening some of the migraine headaches she now had daily.

Muscles melted like ice. Warmth flowed through her, prickling and whooshing. The waves of relaxation she had practiced so often in the past began to come back. She flexed her toes as the waves made her blood tingle then moved to her ankles, where she made small rotations. She flexed her calf, moved her knees in small circles, and rotated her shoulders until she had minute relief from the tension which never went away.

Her mind became a blank slate. *Do with me what you will, Universe. Make me whole, make me rested, give me the strength to take on these quests set forth by whatever destiny needs. Please show me what I need to do.*

"Who is your father?" Grace asked, leaning forward like there was a secret.

"James Skaggs," Kala said as she looked down and massaged her ring finger with her right hand.

Grace stood and began pacing. "Your father, he is Qurban, correct?"

"That is what they tell me." Pangs in Kala's heart took her breath away, sending spasms into her throat. She coughed, lowering her head. Without thinking, she cupped her hands into the water then drank until she had her fill. As an afterthought, she said in her mind, *Bless this water and purify it, Universe. Give me the strength to fight.*

She breathed then looked Grace in the eyes; the sorrow would not defeat her.

Grace waited with a grin, but sadness filled her eyes. "From what I have heard, he is resistant to the control. This Daniel Blood..." She trembled a little at what Kala assumed was the name. "He is resistant to the mutation and the control. They test him daily to see if he can be turned. What if all three of you are a part of this, and your bond will break this cycle?"

Kala scoffed. "We do have a strong bond, but we are weak in magic."

Grace sat back down. "You do not lack in will or love. No matter how they torture you, you go back to wanting to save everyone. But you cannot save everyone. You must have the strength to do harm if there is no other way." Grace looked like she had said too much and bid Kala to rest before going back to her own bed.

★ ☾ ☀ ★

Overwhelmed with her thoughts, Kala knew she would need to spend some energy to stay in a wise space. She hopped from the bed and splashed in the water. Its coldness soothed her achy arches as she walked around, pacing back and forth to warm up the muscles which were rigid from her dream of running and failing. The dream stayed in her head, but she asked her mind to leave it for the moment and focus on her surroundings.

The cell was sixteen by sixteen feet based on her paces and seemed to have that much head space as well. A near-perfect cube which she could not see how to climb. The walls were more like smooth tiles than bricks, with water swirling through them, hypnotic if Kala stared at them too long. The windows in the ceiling were too high up to allow them to jump out. *How can a dungeon be in the basement and still have a window in the ceiling?* There was no way to ask now, as Grace seemed to need some space. Kala needed her own space to think, too.

What was she to do about her situation? She had a feeling she was only in this cell for the short-term. Carl would use and destroy her over and over for his amusement. She wished she could have hidden her ability to heal overnight. The last thing he had done with his tools had not healed like she would have hoped and opened every time she even sneezed too hard. The worst thing was the thought of disappointing Daniel after that; she couldn't imagine *wanting* to be sexual again.

She could worry about that later. She needed to think.

Kala began to perform squats, lunges, and jumping jacks. Her wounds did not reopen, and her spirits lifted. She hadn't practiced Muay Thai in a long time, but she knew the motions, so she started slow. Jab, Cross, Jab, Cross, Cross, Uppercut and then another, following with hooks and a variety of kicks. She wanted to make sure she knew them all.

She practiced for hours. Her neck tingled as Grace watched her. Sweat poured from Kala's body. She seemed to rehydrate without drinking, though she didn't stop to consider how. Her motions became more fluid; she was the water, striking out as a wave, crashing down with her elbow on an imaginary opponent. Her last jab sent shards of water from her fist, which impaled themselves into the opposite wall. She examined them; they were fluid inside and seemed to be coated with glass or resin.

Grace applauded and sat down in the water, as graceful as a swan. Kala joined her, glad to talk again. Everything confused her.

"Tell me about your childhood," Grace said.

Kala hesitated, caught off guard. How did that relate to what was happening? "What do you want to know about it? I was a child for a long time."

Grace laughed, and Kala couldn't help smiling at the sound, reminiscent of singing while gurgling water. "What did you like to do when you were a child? What did your father do with you? What did you want to be when you grew up?"

"I liked to do anything I could, as long as I could learn. Horseback riding, playing with and caring for animals, singing, drawing, writing silly poetry and stories, running, swimming... although I wasn't fast, and my form was sloppy... I was a hurdler in track."

Grace cocked her head to the side in question.

"I overcame obstacles, created by people for sport, running one hundred and three hundred meters."

"That must have been daunting. How high were the hurdles?" Grace leaned forward, elbow-deep in the water, almost standing on her hands.

"Each hurdle came up to my thigh, or somewhere around there. They were daunting at first, but once I learned what I was doing, they became fun. I was excited when I was chosen to run them."

"You do not jump the hurdles?"

"No, not really. I would run fast enough to use kinetic force to push me up a little as I extended my leg." Kala demonstrated.

"So that is a sport?" Grace seemed breathless, like sports were unheard of.

"What do you do here for fun?"

Grace sighed and looked down at her hands, which were cupped together in her lap. Kala saw it as a sign of respect, like she had seen in other cultures. "I have been locked away here since Abeja was overthrown by Carl and the Qazanat. I do not know how much time has passed, but I have not enjoyed myself in so long, I do not recall fun activities."

Kala thought for a moment and sat facing Grace. "What if we create our own game? We could figure something out together, I'm certain. Something we could play together or by ourselves as a fun practice."

"What a wonderful idea!" She looked around. "All we have is water and our stone beds."

"We could pretend we're sharks and eat all the bad guys, then spit them out because they are gross. The beds will be the safe zone, where we can throw magic at them."

Grace laughed so hard she fell back, and Kala wondered if she was acting already. "That is marvelous. We would not have to split our forces."

"Indeed. Let the resistance begin now."

Kala had the *Jaws* theme in her head every time they played that game... Dun-nuh ... dun-nuh ...

The guards came daily after that. Instead of taking her to Carl, they took her to an interrogation room which was filled with sprinted. She decided to be careful and walked with speed, remembering to look around corners.

Once, they came upon a Qurban, who also seemed to be hiding. At first, Kala didn't know what to do, but her instincts told her to talk to him. He was a young man, but she did not feel the anxiety she always felt around men this age range. Anyone between twenty and forty-five had bothered her previously, no matter where she went, with few exceptions. She could tell this man was struggling and she wanted to help. It was a compulsion; she needed to help. That need wouldn't be denied.

Grace attempted to pull her back, but Kala moved forward.

"Are you okay?" she whispered, still at least five feet away from where he was hunkered.

He jumped and turned, fists raised.

"It's okay, I won't hurt you."

"Who are you?" he asked, looking back and forth between Kala and Grace. He inched away as he spoke.

"I'm Kala Skaggs."

"It's you! Daniel Blood, you're his woman, right?"

"His woman," Grace scoffed.

Kala made shushing noises, though they were just as loud.

The man bowed to Grace. "Princess Grace…" It sounded funny to call Grace Princess Grace, but Kala thought it would have been rude to laugh.

"Yes, and you are?"

"I am Slimad Huntington, Your Grace. I was attempting to escape, but I hit a wall. I haven't been able to get past it."

Kala thought she knew what this was. "Are you under Carl's control?"

"I do not know. The Qazanat… did things to me. I did not know it had worked, until now. My group left me, and I have not found another way out." He looked at Kala. "You smell nice, like home."

"What?" Kala stepped away from him. He looked down at her blood on the ground and crawled toward it. "Are you attracted to my blood?"

The man looked shocked then pulled himself away. "I am sorry, I did not mean harm. This has never happened before."

Kala closed her eyes. It was the only way she could think right now.

She felt energy forces surrounding her. Grace stood just to the right, close enough to defend them both but far enough away to give Kala space. She could even feel Grace's height, the exact same height as herself. They truly could have been twins.

She wondered if there were others in other lands just like her. But their energies were different. She could feel it now; Grace was calm under pressure, Kala was a raging storm just waiting to erupt and destroy everything, whether she intended to or not.

The area seemed hidden; only a few people must know where it was. "You stay here, Slimad. Grace and I must go; we will come back for you if we can, but I feel it is safer if we are apart until I have figured this out." Slimad obeyed, but nonetheless Kala looked back often. He did not move from the spot, just stared at the wall across from him. Eventually he sat down on the water-soaked floor, saturating his clothes. "Why do they get clothes while we are nude all the time?"

"I do not know, but I am getting used to it. Before this, I would have been shamed had I shown my ankles. Now, being naked is the best of the worst."

"I know what you mean. It almost seems like I'm used to bleeding all the time and being bruised and battered. I may look healed from my natural ability, but it feels like all the wounds I've

Would there ever be joy in this place? She couldn't imagine feeling happy here. In her mind, she hoped never to come back once they had defeated their enemies. She wanted this weight to lift, the torture to be over. Everything seemed pointless. Why would anyone want people to choose death?

It seemed like she had asked this question too many times and would ask this question over and over until she received an answer or died.

"I don't know how much more I can take," Kala whispered, staring in the direction Slimad went. "The more I learn about this place, the more it seems I'm the cause of its pain."

"This is not your fault, Kala Skaggs. A wise woman knows when not to take blame."

Kala laughed; the hollow laugh trapped in her throat. How could she laugh at a time like this? She knew how. She needed to. For the hope of... It was weird to think she could help humanity.

"I won't know what I'm to be blamed for until I know what I've done or haven't done. I believe I will find answers when we find Daniel. That's how it always works with me; he knows how to help me navigate the mind traps. He helps me see me as I am, not as I see myself."

"Then let us find him. Feel him and lead us to him. Be quick though. It has been too quiet for too long. I fear the worst."

Kala couldn't agree more. She closed her eyes, noting the hard feeling in her chest and her throat. It was as if she was scared to breathe, or to feel. Either of those could help her or harm her, and her mind chose survival most of all. She hoped she wouldn't be the only one surviving by the end.

12

"Focus your mind, Daniel."

Sonaria's voice grated on his nerves. She had been telling him to focus without end, giving him no time to find his focus. He knew what she was doing. She was trying to push him to use his powers during distractions. Too bad she hadn't accounted for his anger over everything. Focus was impossible.

"Shut up for a minute," Daniel growled. He grabbed the canteen by his side and poured water down his throat. He couldn't look at her. He needed her to go away; *he* needed to get away. A dock formed and the water called to him. He pulled his guitar out of its case and began to play.

"Where did you find your guitar?"

Sonaria was right. The case wasn't on the ground, it was in his mind.

"It was just there." Daniel plucked at the strings, which were tuned to perfection.

"What did you think before you grasped your guitar?"

Daniel stared down at the guitar; he pressed a strange button on its head. The acoustic guitar transformed into the most interesting musical weapon he had ever seen. Its bridge was covered in piano-like keys which plucked at eight strings. The guitar's body was shaped like a flaming ax, its edge twinkled in the sunlight. It would never need sharpening. Or cleaning. The knowledge came from within him. "I needed to get away."

"You did it! You used the Void to harness your power. Brace yourself. Now the real training will begin."

Daniel did his best, but his back twinged when he moved; pain shivered down his spine so he could neither bend nor twist. This magic was all twists and bends—it felt impossible right now, or ever. His fingers clamped and clawed at the instrument.

"Stop lashing out. That weakens you."

"How am I lashing out?" Daniel was angry at himself, not Sonaria. He couldn't think, couldn't focus on the task.

"When angered, you send shards of energy through the air. They do nothing except cause jitters, and your energy depletes faster than if you sent a full shock wave of music through the air. Menacing does nothing for the Warrior Empath. You need to be calm, collected."

"Useful," Daniel added.

"Yes, useful," Sonaria said with a smirk. "Everyone needs to be useful at some point in their life."

"Why am I here? Why am I training for a fight that is not my own when I've been fighting all my life?" How could someone hold onto hope when the world continued to crash down around them?

"The world needs your guidance. But you cannot fulfill your task until you learn more."

"What task?"

"Eventually? You will train to defeat someone who has never been defeated. It will take all the Empaths of the worlds to defeat him, and you three will lead them."

"Psh… That's crazy. Kala is the Empath, not me."

"You are both Empaths. Kala is the Healing Empath, you are the Growth Empath, and James is the Magnetic Empath. All three of you are warriors. All three can learn to wind whisper; you already show potential in that area."

"What is wind whispering?"

"It is a power most common in those from Howaja, the land of air and clouds. It works with directional magic, which James possesses—I see he ignited your directional potential—the ability to send spells or messages far away."

Daniel shrugged and shook his head. It sounded like an insecure means of communication. "Can the messages be intercepted?"

"They could, but the interceptor would be unable to hear the message. The wind whisperer must have a specific individual in mind."

"That could come in handy, if I can learn it. Now, what was I supposed to be doing?"

"You are learning to soothe during stress. If you can do it here, you can do it anywhere."

"We'll see about that." Daniel put his back into the twist and smiled. He could move again and somehow felt freer knowing he would have helpers this time around. He needed to soothe because Kala's life depended on her sense of security, for which he felt responsible.

His own life depended on the ability to sleep. If he learned this power, he knew he could sleep, and then he would find Kala in his dreams again. They needed one another.

As Daniel fell to the ground, she raced to him, forgetting everything except him. She felt for his pulse, his breath. His energy was weak. Was he losing his spirit? His hope?

No, he can't die, she thought, breathing through the tension in her throat. She couldn't tolerate the heavy feeling of faltering hope deep in her heart.

She focused on turning the tension into a healing glow; the energy moved through her breath.

She leaned towards Daniel, breathing into his mouth. Laying her hand on his chest, she drove her energy into him, hoping it would have the same effect as CPR thrusts. His back popped, then his ribs; she saw his body adjust. He slept, breathing easily. She curled along the length of him, smiled at Grace, and brushed the hair out of his face.

Sweat coated his brow and she wiped it away. When she put her hand on the ground, sand stuck to the sweat. The grit didn't bother her. In her heart, she was home, and she would enjoy it while it lasted. Who knew what would come? *Be happy in yourself and learn something every day.* She was doing that.

Kala watched as Grace sat on the dock and looked out at the sea. On the horizon, the sun contrasted with the purple and navy-blue sky, filled to the brim with stars and four moons. The Void felt like a dream, one where you could control what happened. *Could everyone use it like this, or did the Void choose who it would listen to?*

Night fell. Grace stayed on the dock, but Kala was tired. She envisioned a blanket and pillow for each of them. Grace's pillow and blanket appeared on the dock—and they slept, safe within the Void, able to relax and hope and dream.

★ ☾ ☼ ★

Daniel stood beneath a weeping willow. Its bedraggled leaves brought tears to his eyes, though the tree was healthy and its life filled him. He had a motivation, the most important motivation in his life. He would protect those he loved and destroy those who sought to control the worlds.

He stopped for a moment, wondering where he had got this knowledge. Sonaria had not said much, and she had disappeared the moment he felt Kala.

How had he not realized before? Sonaria had said Kala didn't know herself, but he knew her. She would find him under this tree and share what she knew, just as he would have.

Kala appeared, and she sat with her eyes closed, her back against the weeping willow. He gasped when she opened her eyes. They were bluer than he recalled, bright and focused. He could see she was disconnected; it was as if a pane of bulletproof glass pushed the color back into her head. The light from the glass penetrated him, and he sighed with ecstasy. They were together again, both alive and well-ish.

She stood and walked to him. She was fitter; muscles in her abs stood out as they hadn't before. He had always loved the way she looked, but this new strength flowed from her and through him. He felt no pain in his body, which was asleep in the Void.

"I've missed you," Kala said. She looked down and touched the abs in his stomach. "You look better in this dream. But I saw you in the Void. You seemed... frayed at the edges. What have they done to you?"

"What have they done to me? Everything they could, short of killing me. I saw..." He looked into Kala's eyes, knowing she hated the name. "I saw Carl." She didn't flinch. "I wanted to kill him."

"I think they're trying to get me pregnant," Kala said, her eyes widened. "Shit, I don't know if they are, but I need to put up a shield for that again. Hold on." She closed her eyes and assessed her body. "Nope, no pregnancy. Good. Protect me from the Qazanat, Universe. Do not let their plans come to fruition."

Daniel cringed at the prayer-like words then sighed. "Whatever they are planning, we will get out. I don't think they want to kill us."

"That's strange," Kala replied as she opened her eyes. "Well, if we aren't going to die, I want to live." She smiled. "Are you up for some extreme cuddles?"

"You want that?" Confusion sparked his uncertainty.

"I want *you*. They can force themselves on me, but you have my heart. I will not let them destroy what we have. In my dreams, I feel no pain. I want this."

"Deal! I love you, Kala. Let's teach them a lesson."

In the dream, they spent hours making love. She sounded like she enjoyed it, which excited him even more.

They did what felt right and he stopped thinking. Her eyes drew him in, so fierce and wild. She wanted him with all her being, and he wanted her the same. What stopped them?

The glass wall in her eyes melted away and she became whole. He joined her in wholeness. Being together in this moment felt right. And in this moment of crisis, both needed several escapes. This would be his, and theirs.

Afterwards, they lay in one another's arms and Kala told him about Grace, this princess who was not Kala. They discussed what they knew, and Kala was able to talk about her traumas more easily than before, though he suspected she couldn't recall everything. Memory problems were common for her.

He wanted to cry. But he could see something new: she was a fighter, not just a survivor.

He sighed and melted into Kala's arms. Their legs tangled together as they lay underneath the moons. Why were there four moons there? Was it a hint? They could discuss that tomorrow.

His heart continued to burn with rage, but he let it go for now. Karma would make Carl its bitch, and they would walk away, forever.

emanated from her. She wouldn't hurt Kala and neither would Daniel.

What was wrong with her?

Kala sighed and sat down hard enough to cause her butt to bounce on the ground. With an "ow", she gritted her teeth and sighed again, this time louder. She had to activate the vagus nerve to calm herself, which she knew she could do through a yawn or "arr" sound.

She wanted to sing, but experience had shown she was unable to sing in a vulnerable state. Tension pressed on her windpipe; the muscles moved out of the way. Intrigue set in. Kala studied how she felt.

Pressure in her head sent waves of panic into her and she settled them with slow, deep breaths. Her breath shook and she knew why: the putrid scent of Carl filled her mind. His eyes were all she could see. Their sewage-like color mirrored his scent. Could eyes show a person's soul, like some cultures believed?

Shivers overtook her, shaking her from head to toe; cold permeated her marrow. With another breath, she focused deeper. The pathway from her lungs to her brain was blocked by tension at the base of her skull. That explained why she could not think in a straight line.

As she held her breath, the nerves activated in her mind; her brain stem fired up and her vision cleared.

"Kala? Are you okay?" Daniel shook her and the force jogged her back to the moment.

"I'm okay. Just a panic attack—nothing I can't handle." She chuckled and then sighed. The chuckle sounded forced, even to her.

"It makes sense to panic. You're in a safe place here. Take your time."

At the same moment, tremors shook the ground and the lake turned red. "Blood magic." Grace gasped and ran for Kala. "We must hide you both."

"No, I won't hide," Kala said.

"There's nowhere to hide," Daniel said at the same time. They smiled at one another. At least they were almost on the same page now.

"I have a plan... well, kind of." Kala looked around to make sure no bad guys were there. "I'm gonna make Carl wish he'd never been born." With a laugh, she said louder, "That line's so cliché, isn't it?" The Void crashed down and darkness filled the space.

Kala smelled iron and laid in a pool of blood which was not her own. Again.

Fear gripped her, and she looked around. Had she sensed this and taken it out on Daniel and Grace? That must be it.

The enhanced drama filled her insecurities to the brim, but she took hold of herself. She would not hide, nor would she cower.

"Daniel?" It was dark, but she could hear his breathing. He was in pain, and she felt his pain. It went deeper than the skeletal system; something magical affected him.

The lack of light did not deter her. With a breath, she drew the light from within her and she glowed as she had in her dream so long ago. The Void, once beautiful and vibrant, resembled broken stained glass. Her light penetrated the tiles and sent bright shards around the three of them, protecting them from harm, at least for a short time.

The light flickered; she was new at this. But it came back to her. She opened her heart to Daniel and Grace. The light grew around them and she called on the wind like she had practiced before she had even known she was magical. As she breathed, she pretended she was the wind, pretended she was the light.

How would light think? Perhaps it would want to show all the beauty in the world to others. Perhaps the wind wanted to spread the seed of calm to the world or send seedlings to travel and grow in a new environment.

She smiled.

Daniel looked right at her and growled. "You did this…" he said through clenched teeth.

"No, Daniel, I didn't. Look up there!" She saw what she was pointing at right as she pointed. Then she felt it; Carl was in the room. "Blood magic was used; I can feel it. The air reeks of sulfur and iron."

At her words, Daniel shrank to the ground. "I'm sorry. I wanted to kill you right then."

"It's okay," Kala said. She knew what it was. "Carl has extreme compulsion abilities. It took me a long time to see it, but I know now. I have been controlled my whole life, up until I met you. I will not use my newfound strength on you, I swear."

"Why would you say it like that? Now I'm thinking you might." He looked into her eyes and sighed. "No, I know you won't. You won't even hurt wasps who sting you."

"Guess again," Kala said, looking up at Carl. Her stomach heaved and she let it out as a burp.

"Nice one. How did he find us?" Daniel said.

"I don't know."

The lack of tension against her stomach settled it. She was calm. She was fluid. She was the water. Kala stared at Carl, standing where the main door would have been. Now it was just a hole in the wall.

She absorbed the energy from the water as it flowed from the walls. She brought forth her hand and smiled, putting her fury into the energy she would throw.

A jet of water streamed from her hand, boiling as it flew in a torrent towards Carl. He tried to block her mind with his power, but she was ready for him. In her mind's eye the boiling water hit his compulsion, and he fell backwards into the Void itself. His guards would be unable to help him unless they, too, jumped or fell.

Grace had been quiet through all of this but yelped when she saw Carl fall. "Shall we see what is for dinner?"

Kala laughed.

Daniel looked at Grace and asked, "Was that a cannibal joke?"

Grace responded with a smile at Kala. It was strange how alike they looked. "I have learned from the best."

They walked over to where Carl fell, careful not to step on the glass shards with their bare feet. The air still felt like that bastard: cruel, heavy, a fetid dampness that crushed one's dreams and turned them into nightmares. When she reached Carl, Kala turned and vomited—the stench of his essence was unbearable.

Daniel and Grace turned to Kala, and that's when she saw, out of the corner of her eye, Carl stand up. She turned to him just before he did something. Her mind shut down, and she was that robot again. Only this time, she couldn't think for herself. When she tried, she fell to her knees and vomited once again. Her throat screamed for water, for relief. Instead, she expelled every bit of bile from her stomach then fell into the pool of vomit.

The world became black once more.

The darkness dissipated into a memory. She must have passed out.

She was four years old again, in kindergarten. She could read already, before she came to school. She wanted to be smart, but she knew it for what it was—she loved to learn.

Nap time had come, and Kala felt safe. She was in a Christian school and she was sometimes given the option to stay at home and learn. She liked that option; being around people was already a bad thing for her.

She preferred to read on the concrete block that was their front step; the trailer wasn't much, but it was home. Her family loved her, her daddy most of all. She thought of these things as she lay down.

The mat was homemade and reminded her of her momma and her home. She pulled the blanket up and saw in her mind the puppies on the mat as they came to life and cuddled with her. She could sleep.

Kala was awakened by the pastor's adopted son. She didn't like him; he scared her. But he was almost a grown-up, and that made him her boss. He picked her up from her mat and took her into the bathroom.

"I don't have to pee," she whined, but the teenager pulled off her dress and panties. The nakedness didn't bother her; her mom yelled at her most days to put her clothes on. It was his touch. Rough, calloused hands touched her, and she felt tears come to her eyes. She stopped them and glared.

"Stop," she said as she wiggled around, but the boy-man didn't listen.

The boy-man made her touch him. Instead of giving in to tears, she saw herself from behind. She looked up and saw his face. She knew to stay away now.

She heard a noise.

"Don't tell anyone," he said and put their clothes back in order. He led her by the hand—she pulled back away from him, but he wouldn't let go—and addressed the newcomer.

The pastor's wife was her teacher. She eyed her adopted son.

"She needed to go to the bathroom," he said.

Kala's teacher looked at her but must not have seen the horror and pain.

Somehow, Kala knew in that moment she would never be the same again. She was like her robot dog. He had a button to make him work. Where was Kala's button?

Kala awoke from her dream. Tears streamed down her cheeks; it felt as if she was cramped in that box again. But who cared when she had had a dream like that?

No, not a dream. A memory.

The shock of it made her gasp; she didn't have a chance, even before she could remember. She was already being groomed for sex slavery. If what the Qurban said was true, they must have sent that groomer. It was the only thing that made sense. How could anyone be interested in an undeveloped girl who didn't know anything about pleasure and pain?

Fury inside her rose until she could see inside the box. A red glow emitted from her heart, calming her anger, turning it into a form of center.

She now knew who she was: she was a survivor and healer. Whoever had caused her pain had done so because they feared her.

But why? How could someone who cared about everything and everyone be dangerous to them? She had to know more, and the only way she would learn more while she was trapped in this box would be to access her powers.

Which powers did she have? How could she use them? Could she safeguard her sleep, rest, and heal her mind as well as her body, finally defeat the pain, and grow instead of dying inside? She could, and she would. Starting right now.

She focused inward and whispered to herself, "Seal my mind and give me strength. Help me see and heal. Bring me to the point in time when I can break the seal."

They were the right words; it was as if she had accessed them from another memory bank. Whatever it was, if it didn't harm anyone (anyone who didn't need to be harmed, that is), she would accept it. With a sigh, she sank back into a dream, her muscles relaxed in the cramped space.

In this dream, another memory came to her. She was four yet again. This time, a wasp stung her. She didn't feel it, so it couldn't be real. As she stared at the wasp, she noticed something. This poor creature was protecting its home. She must have been sitting on it. Wondering where its home was, she looked around.

It was right underneath her. Had the wasp's home become squished?

She stood and left the rock pile. The wasps in the nest rejoiced, and she played on her swing instead.

James sat in the dark without moving, but inside he moved. His mind felt like those storms he survived at sea, the ones which drove him to peaks of fear, hopelessness… and excitement. The storms were calmer than when he was younger; he was seventy now but they bothered him more.

His chin dropped to his chest and he breathed in the saltwater scent that gave him energy. He could imagine he was at sea. He wished he could share the journey with Kala and Daniel.

While he looked around, he thought about them. They were in danger, and knew less than he, which was not enough. He was used to being trapped, but he hated it for his family. They didn't deserve it like he did.

The day he had survived what his sister could not came into his head, and he sighed, resigned. "Dear Lord," he said aloud, "please grant me the courage to see this through, and loan me your power so that you can send those who flaunt their disregard for human life to the lake of fire. In your name, I pray. Amen."

Relief flowed through him, and he knew he would be okay, and so would Kala. And Daniel, of course.

James was glad Kala had learned what she needed in life. Now she would need to learn her power, and not feel shame. She had been a happy girl when she was a child and teenager, though he could tell that even then she had needed time to think.

From experience, he knew how hard it was to think fast and to make the right decision. How would her newfound powers affect that? Would she be reckless like she used to be or centered like she was born to be? She had become his reason for living twenty-five years ago, and she was the reason he was able to fight the Qazanat's mutation.

His job was to guide her, and though he had tried, he felt he had failed.

He would not fail again.

The cell where they held him was cold, but he didn't mind the cold. He had some clothing, which was more than he could say for Kala. An odd, stinging sensation occurred when he saw her; she what she was wearing. An adult version of the Garfield pajamas she had worn when she was a child. He smiled and she smiled back.

"I've been called stubborn too. It's okay. You know they aren't right."

Kala looked into his eyes. "No. We are stubborn, and that's what will help us defeat the rat bastard!" She stood and said, "I don't want to cut our time short, but I must heal the others. It's the first phase of my plan, and I must practice."

"Do what you need to do, Kalabear. Oh, and one more thing..." Kala turned to him again. "I approve of Daniel. He's right for you."

"Me too," she said with a smile and was gone in a flash of light. He turned back to the sea, a new purpose in his mind. He too would learn and grow, and help other Qurban. He knew how to control his urges on most days; maybe that's how he could help. He saw Selemati every day—Selemati would learn first. James closed his eyes and floated in space, free to dream of days he had not dreamed of since he was fifteen.

14

Kala awakened in the box with a positive mindset. Her jaw relaxed and she sighed. This confidence was what she had needed most of the time when she had failed. She would not fail; she might stumble, but she would always get back up.

She breathed and lit herself up—a blue radiance—and the inside of the box glowed bright. She adjusted some of the light, worried that it might be seen outside of the box.

The energy from the box pushed against her like a magnet. Its walls beckoned to be saved. The floor, the bed, and even the tainted energy that was Carl hit the light, but she denied his power.

She laughed—Carl was snoring and talking in his sleep. She could not make out the words, but his voice seemed tortured. *How can I laugh at another's pain? That makes me no better than him.*

No other sound came from the room. She focused her mind on the walls of the room, breathed in the light, and whispered, "I am water, I am waves. Let me travel through the walls today." She said it three times. A part of her still winced at her silliness; she was a walking Hallmark card at times. But with a soft giggle, she stepped from the box and into the wall.

She was free of the box. The first step was complete!

Now she needed to find Daniel and James. She also needed to talk to the other captives. She could not save them if she did not get to them.

Daniel, if you can hear me, I am walking from cell to cell tonight to talk to the women and girls. Hope needs to show its face here.

She walked on and heard Daniel in her mind. *Do what you need. Knowing you are safe, I will be fine. I have a plan of my own.*

What is it? she questioned.

Not now, later, he replied.

She recalled something about him; he was a doer, not a talker. *I love you, Lucky. Let me know if you need me.*

I love you too, Speedball. Give them a dose of your kindness!

Kala's smile remained as she climbed down through the walls between the stairs. This was more of a workout than she had anticipated.

She could not recall the last time she had slept well. The fatigue hit her and she fell, skinning her knee. She held the wound until it stopped stinging, then looked at it. The top layer of skin was off, showing red skin that burned as if she had landed on a stripped wire. It wasn't a great start to her plan. Still, she pressed on.

She needed to check on Grace first. She hadn't heard any news about her and imagined different scenarios; the Qazanat tying her up and letting the guards feast on her fought to be top in her mind. These Qazanat were sick in the head. Anything was possible.

"Grace," Kala whispered when she walked through the wall to their cell.

Grace jumped from her bed and raced to Kala, splashing more than she had when they played their shark game.

"Oh, you're alive! I feared the worst!" Tears stained Grace's face and Kala wondered if she looked that puffy when she cried.

"I feared the worst about you, too! I've heard from Daddy and Daniel. They are both alive, and I think they are working on their own plans. Oh, I am so excited! Damn, I haven't rambled like this in so long. I'm nervous…"

Grace shushed Kala and said, "You will do well. Look at how much you've learned on your own! Where is he keeping you?"

"In his room, in the box," Kala said with a grimace.

"Ick, that man is sick."

"I have an idea to change that."

When Grace scoffed, Kala harrumphed, and they laughed.

"No, I'm serious," Kala continued. "I'm a healer. I know psychology, to an extent. I understand emotions and possible outcomes. Why can't I help a person change their brain? Help them become whole? I don't mean right away, by the way. Unless I can find a way to defeat Carl, I can't alter my fate and escape from being chased my whole life."

Grace bowed her head. "Your words speak to me. I cannot sit aside any longer, please let me join you!"

She jumped up and down as she grabbed Kala's hands. The excitement infected Kala, who found herself jumping along with Grace.

They hugged. A blue light formed between them, at heart level, and for three seconds their hands were as one.

"Whoa, what just happened?"

"I think our powers joined. Can you do this?" Grace placed her hand under dripping water and closed her eyes as she collected the droplets. The droplets turned into a clear globe which emitted a blue light.

"That's just it. You must trust all of you, not only your mind. Be comfortable with yourself and you will get it."

"Okay, enough procrastinating…" Kala closed her eyes and breathed. In her mind, she tried to comfort herself, but nothing seemed to work.

You can do it, Kalabear. James' voice traveled through her senses, landing in her eyesight. She could see his sound waves as colors and yellow light. He remained on the boat, and she guessed he was doing the same thing as her–analyzing things to death until they made no sense, then knocking some sense into himself. This would happen in his head, of course.

With a smile at Grace, Kala stepped into the water wall. It was different this time. She could feel the whole castle, its life, its breath. An urge to swim came over her, but she stepped sideways instead. She considered knocking, but that would be silly for multiple reasons. For one, she assumed no one knew she had this power. Two, they were sneaking. Knocking on walls and doors was one step below bellowing their names, motives, agendas, and weaknesses. She stepped through, and her breath stopped at what she saw.

A little girl, no more than eleven, lay on the only bed in the cell. A woman, who appeared to be her mother, sat on the bed with her, cradling her head while singing a lullaby Kala didn't recognize.

"Oh, no! Sammi," Grace said as she moved forward.

Kala reminded herself not to freeze in moments like this.

She looked at the woman and Sammi. There was a visible energy around them; yellow surrounded the woman and yellow with a black core surrounded Sammi. The mother was just as injured as the child, but she would not let the child see her wounds.

"What happened?" Grace asked. The woman looked up at Grace then Kala and gasped.

"You have a twin? How have you kept that secret? Gul would have told me if she had known."

Kala recognized the name. "Gul? That name... did she help James Skaggs?"

"Yes," she said with a sad smile. "It is a shame he is married. Since losing her Patrick, Gul has been fond of James."

Kala closed her eyes and sensed the room. The rising anger provoked too much pain. She wanted to heal instead of getting mad about situations that she couldn't change.

Kala focused on the present. "The little girl, is she your daughter?"

"Yes, this is Sammi."

"What happened before she became this ill?"

"She was taken from me... for..." The woman sighed and lowered her head. "No one is immune; they torture young girls, expecting them to act as adults."

Kala's memories began to surge... four, fourteen, eight, eleven, and many other ages, ones of her own and from others. All of them seemed foreign and familiar at once. She saw herself caught in these acts and shivered. "I know what she's been through. I also feel her pain on top of my own. She's given up; her pain is too much. May I attempt to heal her?"

"Heal? What is this?" She looked at Grace.

"Oh! I forgot to say... She's the Foreseen, a link in the Roshanra." Though it was a whisper, the words echoed through the cell and what seemed the entire building.

Kala felt Carl's body stir in his sleep. How could she feel him right now? Did he have a hold on her brain? Shivers rippled across her body and she swayed but caught herself.

"I need to be quick. I think Carl will awaken soon; I need to be in that box when he wakes." Kala placed her hand on Sammi's belly and two fingers from her right hand on the center of Sammi's forehead.

Bring to me a healing spell that will keep her calm as well. She needs to know hope lingers still… today her soul will heal.

The universe granted her request. Hope flowed from Kala, from the manor, from the world. Every bit of anguish she felt became a healing power, one that affected more than just Sammi.

She felt the power flow through to Sammi's mother, to Grace, to the people in the next cell. To the building itself. A part of her mind told her this secret would not be found. The manor would protect her, just as she tried to protect its residents.

"Oh my," the woman said as Sammi rose, smiling. "Thank you! Thank you!" She hugged Sammi then kissed Kala on both cheeks and on her forehead. "I am forever in your service. Before you leave, I must tell you. I see your strengths. This is but one strength you have; you seem to cultivate them all. In all your energy centers, I see… your fears blind you to the truth. Find the truth you are blind to and it will be yours."

Yay, another riddle. Kala smiled and introduced herself. The woman introduced herself as Angela Pittington.

As Kala and Grace went back to their cell, Kala pondered meeting a new friend, a connection to the woman who had taken her father to safety. She owed Angela her own thanks, but until she found the right words, she would say nothing.

A siren screamed in her head. Knowing what it meant, she sprinted through the water, climbing faster than she had in her life.

She made it to the box but was still panting when Carl opened the door. The anger on his face frightened away any concept of hope, any memory of healing, and any possibility of escape. The tree that had once glowed bright in her mind fell over and died. She was doomed.

Carl grabbed a fistful of Kala's hair and pulled her out of the box. Her neck twisted and popped, but he didn't stop there. He beat her to a pulp, leaving no part of her body unblemished. Blood streamed from gashes where her skin couldn't handle the pressure. She wanted to run but couldn't even sit up straight.

Carl put two glowing, red bracelets on her. The moment they were on her wrists, she felt her power drain from her. The bracelets shone brighter and they tightened, digging into her skin.

Blood poured from her wrists. She stared at the liquid and felt nothing but agony, it grew with each passing second. She slumped against the box. *If I could just get into the wall, I think I could escape him.*

She closed her eyes and tried to breathe. A strand of knots formed from her brain stem all the way down her spine, front and back. Her heart thumped faster, trying to process the tainted life source. Then her heart slowed, exhausted.

"What did you do, you scum?" She couldn't manage more than a whisper.

Carl said nothing. Instead, he smiled.

Kala's blood seemed to coagulate in her veins. She fell, landing on the hard tiles. In a daze, she saw the water tile reach toward her, but she could not reach out for it. Carl laughed and pulled her up by the hair again. He took his knife and placed it at her throat, where he drew a symbol with the point—the symbol seemed to be a teardrop. What was the point of that?

"You will do whatever I say, when I say it. All who you love will die, but you will live as my slave queen."

Kala felt her heart seize, a single tear fell from her eyes, and she entered a deep sleep full of dreams and memories.

15

D aniel sat in his cell and embraced his own darkness. He felt the connection between Kala and himself splinter, and then it shattered. She didn't disconnect from him; the break was forced. Daniel feared the worst—he saw how obedient the Qurban were, and they hated Carl as much as he did.

Somehow, Daniel had escaped the compulsions. At the same time, he blacked out each time he came around a powerful force of evil. He saw in his rage what he could do and longed to finish the task.

Images of each Qazanat member formed in his head, exploding as he approached them. One action against him or any innocent— by innocent he meant non-sadistic people—in the world and that person would die. The image of brain matter dripping from noses satisfied him, but not for long. *This thinking is unproductive and evil. Marine mode, dammit, I need to stop this.*

In his anger, he knew he needed sleep. He had no blanket, but he had his music. A tune bloomed in his head and he followed it until he was lulled to sleep.

Dreamland was dark, but he saw a light up ahead, dim but visible. It was Kala's light.

He raced to it, amazed at his speed. He hated running but loved it in this dream—he felt freer than he had in the Void. Was the Void like a gateway drug to dreaming?

Chains bound her from head to toe. She slouched, and drool ran down her chin and chest. Her hair, disheveled and knotted, dulled in comparison to normal. She stared at a distant point; she didn't seem to see him.

"Kala?" No response.

He screamed and gritted his teeth as he wrestled with her chains. His back spasmed and he readjusted. Each time he pulled, she slipped further away inside her mind. He needed to find her a safe place, a place where she could escape the blood magic. The Kala he knew would disappear forever if he didn't find a way to help.

"Kala. Remember the Void? We saw into each other, and I can still see into you. Fight this!"

Kala's eyes flickered in recognition. A surge of excitement rushed through him, but he didn't trust that feeling.

"Sonaria told me you didn't know yourself while I trained in the Void. Ask yourself, who are you? What do you value? What power do you have and what power does *he* have over you?" He held his breath, jaw clenching as tears ran down his face.

After a few seconds, Kala blinked. Tears fell, and she looked at him. "Daniel? You're alive? Oh, thank… well, I don't know who to thank."

"Thank yourself," Daniel said and smiled through his tears. "When Carl attacked you in the Void, you hit him with a spell that knocked him off his feet. He had to be carried and healed with blood magic. Whatever you did will haunt him. He will be distracted for a while. You can use this to your advantage."

Kala smiled in a devious way and his excitement grew, sending chills down his spine. Kala sensed it and her smile widened. "I'm getting out of these chains," she said, and the chains melted away. Her control in the Void must work in dreams, too. All those astral projection meditations had to be part of the reason she had this control.

She gasped at it then jumped for joy when she saw she was free. "Yay! I'm still chained in the waking world... dammit!" She shook it off quickly. "I'm feeling rebellious right now. Wanna make love so hard Carl feels it and dies in his sleep?"

"God, you're sexy!"

"Then kiss me, my true master." Her words sent him into a frenzy, where everything disappeared except themselves. She glowed brighter each moment they were together, and her eyes resembled an ice cave. The effect was more magical than anything he had experienced in the last two years. He saw in that moment; they were right for one another. If not for her, he would not know magic. And if not for him, she would give up on her hopes and dreams.

"I think the Void became part of me," Kala said afterward. "I was there when you woke me. I couldn't handle what happened, so I escaped. I know what to do now. I will play house with Carl and act like he has me under his control. My spirit will watch from the Void, and he will think it's disappeared. From the Void, I can continue to meet with you and affect the manor... I think."

"It's the only idea we have, so it will have to do," Daniel responded. The tension in his muscles loosened enough for him to breathe more easily. "If the Void is part of you, who is Sonaria?"

"I don't know, but I will find out. Meet me in my dreams tomorrow night? I will try to contact Daddy and Grace as well. We need to work together."

With the matter taken care of, they lay down together and counted the stars in the sky, which must have appeared during their intimacy.

"I miss this," Kala said with a sigh. Her hair, now clean in the dreamworld, glowed with a light golden hue. Her eyes had the same satisfied light in them, and Daniel knew she would be okay.

We will have this again, in the real world... No, Kala, don't scoff. We have to find a way to break this cycle."

"I wasn't scoffing, by the way. I was laughing. I'm the hopeful one most of the time. Now I just want to kill all the people who harm us and hug all the people who wish to live their lives in peace and love. I guess I'm no longer a hippy."

"We each have our moments. Let's rest while we can; long days are ahead. Goodnight, sweetie."

"Goodnight, Lucky. By the way, did I tell you I dreamed of you when I was a child? That's why I call you Lucky; you look like the Lucky Charms mascot." She smiled. "I'm so happy we're together, even in this shit."

"Agreed. Now, stop talking and thinking and go to sleep."

Daniel booped her nose and smiled when she giggled. He could feel her pain, and her stubborn nature fighting that pain with her powers. Somehow he could help her save everyone.

With that idea in his mind, he felt at ease, as much as he could anyway. He closed his eyes and was back in his body, but the connection to Kala was back. The light pressure between his eyes led to where she was. He would find her, no matter where she was taken in life. Then all was black, but he was full of fire.

16

The manacles itched so much that Kala wanted to bite at them. Sometimes she did, until one of the guards eyed her. Would a controlled person feel an itch from the cuffs? She wasn't certain but wouldn't risk it. She went back to her chores instead.

The laundry she washed was not only Carl's, but his were the "most important in her eyes…" At least, that's what she pretended to believe. She couldn't use magic, of course.

The washing pool was just past the entrance. She had been too distracted to see it before. It took up close to half of the room, and it was the same whirlpool they had to dump their toilet cans into. The stench reminded her of the poo ponds in Kandahar. At least she had time away from Carl and his posse.

Her hands gripped the black silk shirt hard enough to crinkle the fabric. She needed to calm down. Using her chant of *Aaram bash*, she breathed deep with her eyes open. She had to work nonstop, otherwise she would be beaten. And her ploy would be found out. Her eyes ached and her stomach tensed as she held back her emotions. She wanted to talk to Daniel all the time; he helped her feel good about herself.

She noticed she didn't always mention her father. Was she just so used to him being gone that he was second in Kala's life?

Your husband should be first in your life, after God, of course, James said in her mind.

Right, I keep forgetting we can talk to one another. This job is so lonely! How are you holding up? Do they still force you to watch me?

Yes, they do, from a room behind Carl's. I'm there now. How are we talking now?

I don't know. It feels like wind whispering through my head. Maybe it's an air power. Is there such a thing as wind whispering?

Yes, there is. When we are free, Gul can speak to you about it. You look healthy, Kala. Keep up the positivity. It suits you.

I'm healthy enough, Kala thought to him, though her pain levels were higher than ever. She continued. *But how healthy are you? Do you look like the Qurban now?*

No, and it causes Carl to lose his wits. He's desperate; beware, he may play the wolf in sheep's clothing to find out what you know.

If he tried to be nice, I would see right through it. But I can make something up. Let's see… If Daddy feels trapped, he will never be controlled. How does that sound?

I think he would see you're only trying to free me. Nice thought, though. I'm sure your soul will come up with something; you've always had a vivid imagination.

I gotta go, Kala said. *I think they will see if I'm talking in my head instead of listening to the bullshit they spew. Derrick, the ever-faithful head rapist puppet, is heading my way. He always makes me "perform" for him before he takes me to Carl.*

He will get his comeuppance. God bless you, Kala.

And the universe bless you, Daddy.

★ ☾ ☼ ★

Pretending to be compelled was harder than Kala thought. She had to smile when she wanted to scream. And she was choosing to do so! Her mind replayed the events in her head every night when she slept. Getting to sleep was a problem—would she be raped while asleep again? Would she bleed for days afterwards, with zero days free from at least five unwanted sexual experiences a day?

She walked through the hallways, freer than most, yet more restricted. She knew her mindset was correct. Every so often, she would send Daniel cryptic messages that only he would get. *Moist farts*, she giggled in her mind.

*Snoodleparka*s, Daniel responded.

She could hear worry in his thoughts, yet kindness and faith in her set her jaw to the task. She had to seem relaxed. Truly compelled people would be "happy" in their service. What a load of horseshit! She almost screamed the last but covered it as a yawn instead.

She went to the kitchens to fetch Carl's lunch.

Kala wasn't allowed to eat every day. She was "too fat for his task." She gripped the tray with both hands. White knuckles reminded her to calm down.

Aaram bash. She was the water, the coral, the pearls, and trees. She was the air, the hope, the passion for life and love. She reminded herself of this daily; it finally worked! She was as calm as the water itself. But inside, she calculated every move of every person, found ways to poison the guards without coming near— that was a simple matter of grinding the poison to a thin powder and using her air power to deliver the poison in increments.

The tedious process didn't kill the guards, but the women, some at least, had reprieves from their torture. Kala had no reprieve, or so *they* thought. The Void was inside her, and she lived inside it. She was at one with the Void, which connected her to the Universe.

"Hey, slut!"

"Hello, Derrick, it's nice to see you." She writhed inside the Void, and her spirit vomited. Kala saw it in her head; light spewed from the spirit. Could she lose her energy if she didn't escape soon? Is that what they wanted?

"The Master wishes to see you."

"Of course," Kala said. Her sarcasm went unnoticed, or so she hoped. *Don't over-think*, her spirit reminded her. *I will watch over you.*

Derrick ran off, leaving her alone. *That's a first. I wonder what's going on. Why didn't he take me by the arm like normal?*

She was heading back to Carl's room anyway. Why had he called for her? She would go, but she drew the line at running to his side.

As she walked, she noticed her surroundings more. The solid water tiles making up the walls leaked in various places, making it more of a cascading Zen garden than a structured building. The water reeked of the poison of death and brutality... and hope. She wanted to heal it more, but now was not the time. She had to do the tasks assigned by stupid asshat Carl.

Light spilled in from her left. Excited, she looked over. A door she had not seen before remained open, beckoning her to leave through it. She moved closer, examining the door and what lay outside.

Beyond, she saw an ocean, water as far as the eye could see. Rays shot through the clouds and sprinkled the water with glittery sunlight. A stone path led from the door along the sides of a cliff.

"Not today, Derrick," Carl said with a sneer toward Kala. "This one is needed. Now."

"Yes, Master. Where must I take her?"

"To my chamber. She must hang the wash and stand there until it is dry. The normal punishments are overdone, and she is no longer affected by them."

"Yes, Master. Come, scum."

Kala followed in seething silence. She felt Carl's eyes pierce her back and her mind. He was probing. She knew how to recognize it now, which was both eerie and interesting. His compulsion left remnants of his essence's stench, coating her tongue and inflaming the cells in her brain. Pressure built in her hippocampus, amygdala, and prefrontal cortex. Her vision blurred and her eyes dried; a sign that he was stealing some of her power. If she used her powers to block him, he would know she was faking. Well, she would get her strength back, one day.

Each time she walked this corridor, she had seen more. Now she saw less. She was alone, though she felt the essence of each survivor, hundreds of them, all their energies stabbing at her heart like an electric pitchfork.

Sometimes the pains reached her from outside the manor. How far away were they? Could her senses reach miles, or was a rescue team close? She hoped the latter; she had yet to find a way out for everyone.

She refused to leave people to an unknown fate. Somehow, she knew Carl would dispose of them before letting her free them. He was rotten to the core. How could someone have zero good qualities? There had to be some way to convince him to stop this madness. She could see the negativity dragged even his moods down at times. Did she cause that?

Then it hit her. *Daddy, Daniel, Grace... I think I've been healing Carl while he attacks me. I'm not sure, but it seems he's more emotional than before.*

I feel it too, James responded.

Don't trust him, Daniel said, his voice unsteady. The quavering reminded Kala too much of losing her father. Was that an effect of the mutation? Was it getting to Daniel? Her heart beat faster; surely Carl could hear it.

Daniel, are you okay? You seem tired.

No shit, Kala...

No, I mean... has the virus taken you?

No. It's exhausting.

I understand. God, I gotta find a way for us to get out! I think I'm the only "free" one in this place. I feel overwhelmed with the pressure put on me. After we get out, let's take a vacation.

We won't have time, Daniel said. *A few days of rest to figure out what we're doing, then we must do it.*

Okay, I'll figure something out. Tonight, I'll see if I can spirit walk to the library. I also have a few more people to visit... the ones who have been here the longest will need encouragement.

Good luck, they all said at the same time. Kala struggled to keep a straight face but the giggles remained in her mind, allowing her to push through the pain. *One step at a time, take everything I see and feel in, and succeed at my mission.*

Kala arrived at Carl's room and gasped, dropping the laundry. She looked around to make sure no one saw and picked it up. No stains; good. The punishment for stains was watching someone else being tortured. He had found her weakness, for sure. But she knew her weakness was also a strength. So, take that, asshats! Kala knew how to be dialectical… sometimes.

She had to be hallucinating; it was the stress, surely. Yet the air coming toward her told a different story. A window stood open across from her—she didn't even know there was a window in his room—that led to a drop onto a rocky shore hundreds of feet below.

Beyond that, as far as the eye could see, marshes and rivers connected, leading to a huge waterfall that whooshed in Kala's mind. Trees lined the sunset sky which shone through dark clouds that announced the end of the storm. Her spirit put her on autopilot then walked outside while her meat suit remained inside. She hoped the anti-control part of the Void would protect her body. But she had to explore; she couldn't stand back and do nothing!

People were the priority if they were to survive. With a smile, Kala's spirit splashed through the walls and down to the dungeons.

This was the first time she could recall talking to someone in spirit form, yet a vague sense of familiarity rose in her. Did Carl remove her memories? Nervousness filled her to the point where she shook. She could feel it, disconnected but real, so she stopped the anxiety. Even a spirit needed to breathe sometimes.

The first room held an elderly lady. Kala didn't guess her age—most people wouldn't like that—but Kala could see she had lived a long time and through many hardships. She was rail thin, lacking muscle and energy. Her stomach was stretched out, like she had been used as a birthing mule. Dark skin hung under her arms, chin, and in her thighs. The poor woman put off an energy that indicated she was giving up. Something kept her from giving in, however, and that was a sign to Kala. The woman knew what she wanted in life and was determined to find it.

"Hello," Kala said, and the woman jumped. "I'm sorry to scare you. I'm not used to this."

The woman looked at Kala with amazement, eyes wide with tears. "It is true. You are one of the Foreseen, the Healer of the Roshanra. How did you come to me?"

"I spirit walked through the walls."

"You're a spirit? How can I see you?"

"I have no idea. But you can, so that's what matters right now. Do you need healing?"

"Oh, I do not know. I would not want to take away your energy."

"It's nothing. I use the energy of the Universe to transform pains into healing and nourishment. It sometimes helps me. What's your name?"

"Lebase, my lady."

"I'm far from a lady; call me Kala. Please, close your eyes and picture a safe place where you feel warm and free."

Lebase did as Kala asked, and Kala moved closer to her. The energy coming from Lebase grew twice as large as when Kala first arrived, heat coming off her in waves. She had found her safe place.

Kala placed her hand over Lebase's heart and felt it beat. It was strong, stronger than Kala's own. There was a lot of love, a lot of hurt, a lot of hatred, and more than enough shame to drown everything else away. Kala poked at the shame with her mind's eye, opening the bubble that consumed the rest with ease. The pain flowed out and Kala drank it in, purified it through her liver, then sent it back to Lebase as love, hope, happiness, and fulfillment.

Her energy, while powerful and protected, sent waves of nausea into her and caused her body to feel heavy, like she carried her gear to the planes again. Body armor, weapons, a heavy blanket, and all the gear she needed to carry for her task. All in all, it was at least fifty extra pounds… if she didn't underestimate it.

Carl led her down past the dungeons, all the way to the lab, where Daniel and James both sat chained to the wall, their skin sliced off in places. Some wounds bled while others flaked as if scabs had formed and healed under, showing white scars beneath the tick-colored crust which fell like confetti to the water tiles below. She wanted to rush to them but Daniel, warned *No, don't give yourself away.*

James added, *You can stop your impulse, Kala.*

Kala held her breath and saw things for what they were, not what Carl wanted. James was a free man in his mind, as was Daniel. They knew who they were. Since Kala had begun to resist Carl, did she know who she was? It was all confusing, and the more confused she became the more she wanted to help Daniel and James.

Her hand lifted of its own accord. *No, I will not let confusion, anger, and fear drive me. I am willing to let go and be who I need to be. Universe, please guide me.*

She would have to be patient. The universe only answered when the time was right. She would not miss the message.

17

It was sleep time, Kala's favorite time of the day since being brought to the manor. Carl chained her body to his canopy bed, but the glowing red bracelets now did nothing to keep her spirit in her body. That's what made it her favorite.

She chose not to climb out during the day, when tortures were combined with questioning—who are you, what can you do, why do you think you are powerful? Kala's answers were what he would have wanted—I'm no one, I can do nothing, I'm powerless. He thought he was winning.

Kala smiled as she went to the window; he left it open, thinking she was tamed. Carl loved reminding her that she couldn't leave. Her spirit climbed out and explored the world around them. Though she couldn't fly as a spirit, which was silly, she could climb. Down she went, to the cliff which overlooked the waterfall. She sat there, contemplating life.

She closed her spirit eyes and breathed in the mist brought by the vast cascading water. Somehow, despite the traumas, she felt calmer these days. Perhaps she could look at this event as prolonged exposure therapy, even though it was revictimization at its core.

She was stronger than she ever thought possible. Something pulled at her strength. She looked in the river and saw a mermaid, staring right at her. The eyes drew her in, though she couldn't see what color they were.

Kala stood and dived off the cliff, plunging into the icy water without the hesitation she would have had in her body. She was free, which made her feel guilty. Still, her freedom had a purpose.

Her goal was to greet the mermaid whose eyes drew her in. Everyone's eyes drew Kala in, but not like this. She needed to know her, to know about the mermaids.

She landed in the water with a splash and swam to the bottom. In spirit form, she could breathe underwater. She laughed, and bubbles flowed from her mouth and nose. Laughing more, she swam downriver and sent pulses through the water. She didn't know if spirit walking would always be possible in captivity; time was limited. She had to find the mermaid tonight.

Shock waves pushed her back to the waterfall, and the undertow pulled at her. She allowed the water to drag her down, all the while smiling at the fun of it. Her body wouldn't have survived this but her soul reveled in the adventure. That's when the mermaid pulled her out.

"What you do?" the mermaid said. Her heavy accent was hard to understand.

Kala replied, "I sent for you," though it only came out in bubbles. The mermaid laughed and dragged Kala to the bank, where Kala pulled herself out and sat at the edge. She poked her feet in the water. "What I tried to say was that I sent for you."

"How you know I?"

The mermaid's English reminded Kala of her cousin who had trouble with her and she. This was the first time Kala felt homesick, and it drove her spirits down. "I don't know you, but I need your help. Is there anyone who can free captives in Terois Manor?"

"I show you. Come." The mermaid extended her hand and Kala took it. "I Aquin Seafarer."

"I'm Kala Skaggs. It's nice to meet you." The mermaid smiled; her white, pointy teeth glistened in the moonlight.

They walked in silence and Kala took in the view. The high cliffs and the manor receded as they moved, and Kala wondered how fast they walked. She didn't ask, however, and kept looking around. She would need to know the terrain soon. A small forest on the left was quiet. Ahead, another waterfall spilled over a meadow, yet the meadow didn't become waterlogged. The wind wafted the flowers; shades of blues and greens and yellows shivered between the wheat and tall grasses. Purple mountains in the distance appeared guarded with a crisscross of trees. They stopped at the waterfall, and Aquin walked through. Kala followed.

Beyond was a city, hidden from the outside world. Kala hesitated. She hated cities; the energies overpowered her sense of self, something she feared the most. Unable to be herself, she only became prey.

"Zamagia," the mermaid said. "You come to castle. Naomi see you."

Kala followed, kept her eyes on the cobblestone road ahead, and breathed. She blocked her senses; anxiety in her spirit self would surely tip off Carl that she could spirit walk. She was supposed to be under his control, after all.

With her eyes on the road, Kala didn't notice the people staring. She was naked and, if her assumption was correct, she would be

A connection clicked in her mind and she knew the kinship they had. He was of her blood, but she was not of his. Her left fist clenched the ring in her pocket. She knew the moment when its bloody contents had been taken from her. Fury rose within her, and in her mind she commanded that the Qurban run from their masters and hide where they would be safe, until she could help them.

The Qurban who stood next to her jogged away, toward the gate. She saw others do the same. They would be free, no matter what happened. She vowed it as she saw the last one leave. Her spirit walked through the manor and went back to her body; the way out would be clear.

19

D aniel followed James and Kala, aware of their mindsets. He believed he knew some of what Kala was going through. He still regretted the violence in his own life; but he would not share that with her this soon. Her torment mixed with his own. What had happened here was informative, no matter how torturous it had been. He was safe and well; now he could protect Kala. She didn't need to know what he had gone through thus far.

It had been half a year since he had seen her in the Void. Her dream self, or spirit self as she might have called it during times when she practiced astral projection for meditation, looked different from her physical form. Her dream form was just as beautiful as her physical form, yet stronger, solid where Kala looked emaciated. He got little food but she looked starved. They must have given her just enough to survive what she went through. He did not know all the details, but he could see it in her eyes. She had changed. So had he.

this, but she could become stable again once she had a safe place to rest. She looked as though she had not slept in days. He had counted the months, watching as each sun set and then rose again. She had been tortured, just like he had, he was sure. Why else would she harbor so much hatred toward the man she killed?

James stopped ahead of them and waved them forward. They all stooped to get a better view. A small door, about the size of a baby gate, was hidden amongst the water tiles to their right. "Do we have to climb through here?" Daniel asked. James nodded. "It seems smaller than the one I went through earlier."

"Ah, low-crawl. We can pretend we are snakes," Kala said as she laughed. She was acting weird. Something about her was more off than normal. "I'll go first," she added.

"No!" James and Daniel both said at once. Daniel added, "Stay in the formation we have. James goes first, then you, and then me. We don't know what's ahead and you're in no shape to make a decision if danger arises." He felt bad for snapping at her, but she was in that mindset where she would sacrifice herself for everyone. He wouldn't have it.

"Okay, that's enough," James chided. "Kala, he's right. You're in no shape to go first, and we can protect you more than you can protect yourself." When Kala looked offended, he added, "We know magic too, and you are malnourished."

When Kala looked down, Daniel had the urge to hold her again. It was obvious the lack of nutrients and sleep kept her from focusing. Instead of holding her, he asked, "Do you remember what you learned in dialectical behavior therapy? How did you get through your emotions before?"

Kala looked right at him and breathed deep. Sparks flew from her, and he could feel her energy levels rise. She stood taller and said, "Breath is life and love and strength. Alright, let's go." Then he saw it; she was stronger than he had thought.

Kala felt better after Daniel reminded her she knew what to do when under duress. She felt like she needed to explain herself to Daniel and her father. She would never forget how it felt plunging the knife into that bastard's heart. She didn't even want to say his name, a vulgar word in her mind and heart again. He made her feel like she was nothing, but she was something, for sure. A killer. She would be torn apart if she let herself go. Never in her life had she wanted to kill anyone more than in that moment, even when she had protected herself before. She couldn't forgive him; he had threatened to take away everything and everyone that had ever mattered to her. In a way, he had already taken them away.

She still held the dagger in her hand, tucked inside the jacket's sleeve, behind her wrist and forearm. Part of her said she was safe and could pocket it, yet she had to be on guard in her mind. After breathing, she considered it again and stopped before she tried to project the Void. She had an idea of what to do, but she needed to destress first.

"Daniel, Daddy, I need to say something." She shook and decided to put the dagger away, in the same pocket as the ring. "I'm sorry you had to see me take a life. I can imagine what you think of me, and I need you to know... He was the man who hurt me before, during survival training. I could only remember him, not what I learned in life. I was so mad when he threatened you, I snapped. I'm so sorry!" She sobbed again and lowered herself to the ground. Her tears became raindrops which obscured everything around her. Her eyes would not adjust until she expelled all her tears. Finally, she stood up, sniffled, and said, "I'm sorry."

James looked at Daniel, and Kala wondered what they were thinking. Daniel began, "Kala, you did nothing wrong. All three of us have killed someone during a time of war. You may not think of it as that, but we are prisoners of war." He gestured around, indicating everyone in the manor. "A little more personal for you than us."

"He's right," James added. "The pain will warsh away with time. You will heal." Kala chuckled at his slight Indiana accent; it came out when he had other things on his mind. She appreciated their kind words but could not resolve the shame she felt. What kind of person would feel glad they killed someone? A second someone, in fact. She saw the real problem. She had stolen from him more than he had stolen from her. She would live with the consequences, no matter what they might be.

James cut through her thoughts and pulled her forward. "Okay, let's go. We can't get caught." Kala watched as James knelt to the ground and pressed on the small door. "Daniel, when you come through, press the notch next to the inside of the door. That will close it."

"How do you know all this?" Kala asked. Surprise must have registered on her face. She had a hard time remaining stoic.

"I know the owners. I can teach you some things about this world, but not now." Without another word, James crawled into the small space and beckoned for Kala to follow. She lowered herself to the ground and crawled using her forearms and toes behind her father. His knees creaked as he extended his legs. They were performing walking planks as they moved. The hole wasn't tall enough for even Kala to crawl upright, and she was the shortest. While Kala crawled on her forearms with her body low,

James was in a full low crawl, clawing at the ground, dragging his body along, pushing forward with his toes. Both men wore pants and long sleeves. Kala only had her father's jacket, which was just long enough to cover her rear in this position. Her knees scraped on the rough ground, burning as the coral cut her skin.

The cold penetrated her bones through the jacket sleeves. A draft came from the floor, and water lay half an inch deep on the floor. Droplets fell on them. Kala's hair was soaked within minutes, both with cold sweat and freshwater. Her body ached anew, and she feared she would never have peace. What was peace, anyway? She felt she would never know it again.

After an eternity, they stopped. "Project the Void just past this door," James said. "Do you know how to do that?"

"I don't know, but I'll try," Kala responded. She closed her eyes and found her spirit, nestled within the Void, in the back of her mind. *I need the Void. Send it to me, please?* Her brain tingled as energy surged from her into the space beyond the door.

They crawled out of the hole into a dimly-lit arena. Light exploded around them as Daniel climbed out and applause surrounded them, echoing through what turned out to be a stadium, much like the ones Kala had seen in gladiator movies or bullfighting arenas. No people were in the stands, yet she was as much on guard as she would have been if she'd seen a thousand people. More, in fact. How could you fight someone you couldn't see? Still, she removed the dagger from her pocket, which warmed her hand instead of cooling it further.

Daniel raised his eyebrows and scratched his head. "This is the bottom of the Void, isn't it? I thought this part was destroyed." James affirmed by nodding. Daniel looked at Kala and asked, "How do you bring the Void back?"

He hated seeing her this way. She mumbled, so softly he could only hear it as a distant whisper, but he believed it concerned them all.

Daniel shook Kala like she was a rag doll, and she looked up at him, then to James. Tears brightened her eyes and threatened to flow if she didn't find her way out. "Kalabear, what happened?"

She looked closer and said, with tears now flowing, "Are we dead?"

"Dead? No, we aren't dead," her father said.

He appeared confused and scared, but Kala couldn't come up with another explanation. They must be dead.

"Why would you ask such a thing?"

"You died four years ago, then two days ago you came back and I've been in misery ever since. Is this hell?"

Daniel and James exchanged a look, and Daniel spoke. "It's been a y—" His sentence was garbled in the garbage bin of her mind.

She watched through shielded eyes. Three levels of clear, distorting glass panes kept her at a distance, yet she could still feel. Sadness penetrated the glass panes, and she felt her pains anew. The rape, the torture, the fear and depression. It would never end. She must be in hell.

"I didn't like it, but I had to lie to you. I never died… I was changed. A mutation. That man wanted to hurt you. I don't even think he knew you. I want to tell you, but we do not have the time. We must go."

Kala's blood boiled and came to the surface again. "Daddy, no. I need to know what is happening. Please, tell me now, while we're safe in the Void." Why had she said that word? What was going on with her? Something… affected her memories.

"Kala, we aren't safe here," Daniel began, but James interrupted with a hand on his arm.

"Daniel is right, we aren't safe, but I will give you a quick version. These men call themselves the Qazanat. Carl is the son of their leader. He found out that you would thwart them, so they tried to get to you through me. Then you kept gaining power, so they went after Daniel and yourself. The stronger you get, the harder they try to harm you."

Kala scoffed and shook her head. She wanted to laugh but only felt shame. "Powerful, me? Ha, giant case of mistaken identity right there." She had gotten everyone in this mess. She would find a way to get them out. "What did they do to you?"

Daniel looked as if he struggled with his emotions, torn between patience and impatience. His energy both pushed her away and pulled her in. James looked Kala right in the eyes, a fire burning behind the blue eyes they shared.

"They tried to turn us into monsters, but they were wrong about us. A friend told me a myth, that a woman would come to heal the nations, her love would keep her grounded, and her father would guide the way. She believes that we are those three. We must find her now. They have people ready to free those here."

"We can't leave them," Kala said, tapping her foot and moving her fingers as if she was signing her intentions. "There are little girls in here being used as sexual playthings. I can't leave them!"

"You stabbed their leader," Daniel said. "They will kill you if you go back in there."

"Well, I have to do something." She felt in her pocket. "Wait, I have the ring. Maybe I can get the Qurban to free them all. It's a shame it can't control the guards, too…"

"That's the ring?" James said. He jumped up to examine it. "Why would you want to control anything?"

"I don't," Kala said, offended that he would think she wanted to control anything. Her skin crawled at the idea. "I want to communicate with them. I bet we can overthrow the guards because the Qurban seem to like me."

"Yet they kept you locked up here for a year…" Daniel said. He appeared to think she was an idiot. Although…

"Wait, a year? Haven't we only been here for two days?" Her head was pounding and her face tingled with the beginnings of a migraine. This wasn't the right time; then again, when would be the time for a massive headache? She pressed her hand into her right eye and the pressure relieved a little.

She saw the time pass in her mind, and she saw for herself the instances of triumph and defeat. Women and children looking to her for inspiration and being thrown into the Void or nightmare room day in and day out. "The Qurban sneaked me food when I was in the nightmare room and gave me hints about the Void. They're on our side but have been under Carl's compulsions. They are gone, running to safety. I can feel that's the truth."

"She's right. The Qurban and I helped each other when I was imprisoned. I helped them escape." He turned from James back to Kala. "We will save these people once we have the outside help," Daniel said. She didn't know what he meant, but he appeared to understand something she hadn't said. "We aren't abandoning them. We need to learn more before we can do any good. Don't be impulsive… remember?"

Daniel was right; she had to get past the urgency to save people and recognize that she could only focus on it after she had figured herself out. After all, killing one person was more than enough for one day.

They walked past the base of the staircase and found a door, one with spikes on the knob, again resembling a lionfish's body. She thought about touching it, but what if it was poisoned with the lionfish venom? She took out her dagger and cut away the spikes. She heard gasps from behind her when it worked. After all, the sapphire blade did not seem that sharp. Yet it had murdered a man with ease.

The door fell back. They ran into the open.

"What does that mean?" Kala had an idea, that it had something to do with light, since _roshan_ was the Dari word for light.

"You are becoming enlightened." Kala laughed so hard and stopped when she saw the confusion on the people's faces. Daniel looked at her like she was being rude, and James looked concerned about her sanity.

"I'm sorry, my brain is all over the place. I laughed because I don't feel enlightened at all. I feel… confused."

"You are she; I believe this because I see your power, the massive aptitude. Before meeting you, I could only see weakness in others. Your light inspired my growth. You will one day learn what you must, but for now you need help." She looked around and crooked her finger toward someone. A man approached, who carried a sack on his back. "You all need items for your journey. We will meet you back at Terois Manor, but the village seer told us to send you to Bareja. There is a map in the bag; go to the marked location and you will find a man who can help us with the goal Angela said you had."

"I'm sorry, I don't recall much of anything from my time in there, much less a conversation with your sister. What goal did I state?"

"To cure your father."

Kala couldn't stand any longer. She fell to her knees and retched but didn't vomit. She had known her father was a Qurban? How had she forgotten an entire year? What was happening to her, to her mind? Was she crazy?

James leaned down to comfort Kala and Daniel ran toward her, carrying a canteen that he somehow obtained. Kala drank from it and her mind calmed down once again.

"That's a selfish goal right now," Kala said, and looked at James and Daniel. An unspoken question, but she knew what was right.

"I do want to save Daddy, but he is here with me and not in as much danger as your sister." She looked back at the lady whose name she did not know. "I vow to free everyone at Terois Manor, including the Qurban. Do you agree with that?"

Murmurs erupted in the group, and the woman raised a fist to halt them. "I accept, but that means we have to go to another place, plan our mission, before we go. Your escape changed our rescue plans. My name is Gul Teroyal, and I vow to help you with this mission. Should we succeed, I vow to fight the Qazanat by your side."

Kala accepted the deal with a handshake and gave her name, marveling at the similarities between their cultures. They sat down for a meal of bread and a strange yet tasty green cheese, eating as a gigantic family.

Gul's red hair reminded Kala of Daniel, and she had to look at him every time she looked at Gul. He smiled at her on occasion, when he wasn't talking to the men about their hobbies and the war.

"Come with me a while," Gul said. "I would like to talk with you."

Kala nodded and stood with some effort; tension mimicked the whip lashes she had endured. She limped a few minutes before the tension subsided, and she felt okay again. She could feel the group watch them as she left. What did they think of her, of all three of them? She was glad their leader was a woman, someone she felt she could trust, even if she didn't know for sure. When she looked back, Daniel stood against a tree, watching her go with a strange look on his face. She would ask him for a walk when they returned.

They were quiet for some time as they walked, which gave Kala the opportunity to look around a bit more. During daylight, the trees seemed to shine in the sun, which was more intense than she had ever seen. She wished she had some sunglasses; she had to

He did as she asked and saw beyond. A single fish swam upstream, followed by another two. They stopped and looked up when they saw him and waved with their fins. "The fish waved at me."

"Yes, I thought so. These are the first fish we have seen since the Qazanat took hold. I believe your presence is bringing them back. You have a gift. Your natural musical talent combined with your ability to relate to animals. You will be a powerful foe against the Qazanat."

"I don't get it," he said, skeptical about the fish and his powers.

"Read the books in Terois Manor. They will tell you more. Of course, we must conquer them first. Do you think it is possible?"

He looked into her eyes without hesitation. "Not impossible, but it will take a collective effort." She nodded, and they walked back in the same silence as before.

But this time he had more to think about. Could the animals be coming back, as she said? What would that mean for the critters? Would they be safe? He resolved to keep them safe, and maybe Kala could have a pal to cuddle at night.

Her nightmares would come back if they hadn't already. He hoped she could overcome them again, but this time he had doubts. She wasn't telling him even half of what had happened, and he couldn't fathom what kept her sane when she was stuck with that monster for so long. One meeting with him had shown Daniel his character. He recalled how Kala shook next to him in the office, naked and bruised. Blood had remained on the sofa when she stood.

When they arrived back at the fire, Kala was sitting to one side with her father. She shivered with cold but did not approach the fire with the rest of the group. She looked sideways at the men, shying away whenever one crossed her path. He was determined that she would never be alone again. He approached and sat down, said "later" when he saw questions in her eyes. Gul began talking, and he pulled Kala closer to him, holding her and transferring his warmth to her. Her eyes drooped but she stayed awake for the second meeting of the evening.

"We are going with the Foreseen to rescue and retake Terois Manor. It will require every one of us if we are to make it out alive. If we survive this, we will stay there until we figure out our next move. Tonight, we sleep. The planning begins tomorrow and we will leave the next day. The mermaids were delayed; without them, our task will be more difficult."

Gul assigned guard duties and talked to her people just out of earshot. He wondered what they said, but he now believed they would not abandon or betray them, and that was enough for now.

"Kala, are you alright?" he asked for what felt like the thousandth time. He couldn't help it. She still shivered despite his warmth and the clothing. "Are you scared?"

Kala nodded her head. "A little. I keep seeing him in my head, or rather all around me, like he's following me."

"He's dead, Kala," James said. "The dead cannot harm you."

"If I can speak to the dead," she whispered, "what keeps the dead from following me?"

"There has to be a reason," Daniel said. "Why don't you ask the jerk?"

"I can't... People will start to notice if I talk back." She crossed her arms around herself in a hug and twisted her core enough to warm up the muscles but thankfully not enough to look insane.

"What does he say to you?" James asked.

★ ☾ ☼ ★

The next morning came faster than Daniel would have wanted. His back screamed and spasmed, forcing him to stretch before he got off the ground. Kala was already up, pacing back and forth and talking to herself. But he knew it was not herself she was talking to. Her face was red, her brows lowered, a V shape formed between her eyes. She looked like she was trying to push someone away, but no one was visible in front of her. Around her, several of the men were gawking like she was an animal in the zoo. He glared at them before he stood and walked to her.

"Where's Daddy?" she asked as Daniel strode up. "I haven't seen him all morning and you were gone last night when I woke, so I thought you would have a plan."

"I don't know," Daniel said, then added, "How long has *he* been bothering you?" When she gave him a questioning look, he pointed at the invisible space between her and the nearest tree.

"I don't know. It seems like he was in my head all night." Kala pressed her palms against her temples; her pain screeched into Daniel's brain, like nails on a chalkboard. Daniel's head throbbed. Concentrating on the music in his mind, he felt his tension ease. He sent the melody to Kala. She sighed as the pressure released; her hands dropped from her temples and she met Daniel's eyes. "He stopped for a while, but he came back. Stronger than before. I think I can't get rid of him because I killed him," she whispered. Her chin lowered to her chest and a tear fell to the ground. "I'm a murderer. Just one more and I'll be a serial killer."

"You did what you had to in the moment. He was trying to kill us all."

"Not all. He wanted to enslave me more than he already had." She looked back up at him, this time with a look of resolve. "I will defeat him for good one day… as long as I don't go crazy first."

"You mean crazier than you are, silly?" Daniel said with a smile. He laughed at the mock anger on her face. "Come on, let's see what these guys have in store for us."

Kala did as he said, looking around and nodding at the nothingness around her. How many people did she see when she was being stalked by the dead? What could they want? It was bothersome and distracting. He was starting to feel as if he existed less than the ghosts. He shook his head; *that* was silly. As soon as they began walking, she had reached for his hand and she squeezed it in a way that soothed him; he imagined it soothed her. She wasn't a murderer; she was a survivor. She had to see that before she could do her thing, whatever that would be.

And what was he supposed to do? He had been in war before, but never anything like this. It was so… shady. People kidnapping people and trying to mutate them. He shivered at the thought and wondered why his mutations hadn't worked in the way the Qazanat thought they would. He was having issues from it, but not the ones they had anticipated. He would have to speak to that blood specialist if he joined them. Maybe Kala was right and it could be healed. That would be the best option; they would have quite the advantage over the Qazanat.

The planning group had gathered when they arrived. Daniel noticed James talking to Gul in a manner that showed they had known each other for a lot longer than James had let on. She must have been the contact James told him about; their conversation finished with laughter, then he returned to Kala and Daniel. James hugged Kala and reached over her shoulder to shake Daniel's hand; Kala embraced her father in a bear hug.

22

Kala had watched as Daniel left the group. She nodded toward the forest with a smile and James followed. Their part of the planning was done, after all. They would be going in with the hope of staying in power there. Elements of the plan made her uncomfortable; what if some of the Terois Manor guards were compelled? After all, some of the guards had shown sympathy when they had been ordered to bring the women to Carl; she hadn't seen them harm other women either. Only a few had shown ill will towards her or the others during captivity, leering at her like she was an enemy who would destroy their favorite toys.

The forest was darker than she recalled, but she found her way by sensing the man she would spend her life with—if he would have her after she killed not one man but two. A tear coursed down her cheek. Not for the men she had killed but for her soul. How could she be good if she was willing to kill?

James put a hand across her back as they walked, patting her shoulder to console her. She looked up, a silent thank you, and continued down the path. After around ten minutes, her best guess with her time distortion, they arrived. Leaves and wind swirled around Daniel like a tornado, and Kala gasped with a smile. She had always loved watching the tornadoes wind their way down a path. But this one was different.

Music filled the air as the tornado increased in speed, yet it hovered where it was, not moving an inch. She could see Daniel inside it, holding something in his hands. Whatever it was morphed into something useful for their task. Several minutes passed, and Daniel fell to his knees; she cringed and wondered at how he could handle the movements with the injuries from his past. He remained still after the wind subsided. All was peaceful except the sound of a cricket chirping.

"Crickets," Kala gasped. "What did you do?"

Daniel jumped up and turned toward her; he took a deep breath like she had surprised him. "I think I created a weapon. Although I'm not sure if it will work."

"May I?" Kala walked up to him before he could answer. He handed it to her and she felt its energy, which calmed her. Petrified wood formed a guitar, controlled by piano keys. Somehow it curved and split into two sharpened blades, resembling an ax. A loop over the handle resembled a curved musical note, forming a knob at the end, and a portion of polished wood stuck out. "This is beautiful. How did you learn this magic?"

She looked up as he answered. "I didn't learn it. An idea came to me and I wanted to try it. This... right here," he pointed at the portion of wood at the end, "is a lever. Watch." He took the ax from her and pulled the lever around, near his thumb. He pressed it and blue light flew from it at high speed. Music flowed from it as it left. "I created a music bomb, which should calm someone who wants to fight."

"That's brilliant! May I add something to it? I want to try."

"Be my guest," he said, smiling at her in a way she hadn't seen since before they were kidnapped.

She took back the ax and began feeling it. The grain which would have splintered before was smooth while maintaining the texture of wood. The blade was thin yet strong; she shook it to see if it would wobble. It remained still as the tree it had come from.

Kala closed her eyes and breathed in for ten seconds, then out for eleven, holding her breath for a moment in between. In her mind, she chanted *ba da sey fro doo sang sang paak koey sang sang.* It was mostly nonsense, but she didn't judge it this time.

The air flowed past her and spoke to her, offering her hope and health and happiness. She accepted its offer with pleasure, and in her mind wished it for all mankind. The ax vibrated, becoming hot then cold in turn. Kala maintained her grip, though it fought her at every turn. When the vibrating and temperature changes stopped, she opened her eyes.

The ax had changed, smoothing itself more, and the lever had disappeared. Daniel grabbed it back. "What did you do?"

"It should do what you say without a physical command now." Kala waved her hand towards the ax. "Try it."

Daniel took it and held the ax towards the trees. He concentrated, his jaw twitched, and nothing happened...

"You have to relax for it to work. I added a healing component; at least that's what I tried."

Daniel tried again, breathing in and out before he focused. The ball of light and music shot out, bright white mixed with blue. She heard the thud of an impact before a man screamed; they ran towards it to see what Daniel had hit.

"Damn, I should know not to fire a weapon without knowing what's in the background," he panted through gritted teeth.

"You couldn't have known; hopefully, we didn't create a dangerous weapon," Kala whispered. They ran on tiptoes, as noiseless as possible. When they arrived at the commotion, they hid behind a tree, both panting a little.

Beyond the tree, a group of men huddled around another, who appeared confused and disoriented. He sat on the ground, humming a tune which Kala recognized as being Daniel's. The man smiled in a way that suggested he was happy with life. Whatever Daniel had done, he had done it well. Daniel stepped from the cover of the tree to greet them.

"Mordami, is that you?"

The man stood and bowed deeply to Daniel; his demeanor said he was honored to be near him. "Yes, it is I. It is good to see you again. My brother is hurt; could you look at him?" Mordami looked towards the trees then said, "James, is that you, brother?"

James walked out of the trees, pulling Kala along with him. "Yes. I want you to meet my daughter, Kala."

All the men looked up, stood, and bowed. One man, taller than the rest, bowed so low that his head touched the ground. "We heard you have slain the Master. We are forever in your debt."

Kala's stomach rolled at the same time as her head. She sat down without a thought for her own safety. James knelt, concern etched across his face, and Daniel ran to her. "Kala, are you okay?"

"No, I'm not okay. I hate what I did; it's never right. But I saw no other way out. He had me..." She didn't want to finish the thought, much less the sentence. For everyone to know *how* weak she was would only bring pity, and she didn't want or need pity. She needed confidence, and the only way she knew how to get it was to keep practicing being sane.

"What did he have you do?" Daniel asked in a whisper. "It's okay. We're among friends. We need to know what you saw, what

"I saw your whole life when that ball hit me. Kala, you're stronger than you know. If you hone that skill, you can change the world without harming another soul. Gul told me you have truth-seeking potential. Healing and truth, Kala, a wonderful combination."

Kala had to sit down. This was all too much. Before, she had always pushed hard to do her best and was a perfectionist at times. She had been looking for a way to let go. Had she found it? Was the answer to throw truths at people, let them see what's wrong with the world, and with themselves?

"How did you become the first Qurban?"

"Selemati explained something to me. He was forced to create a mutation based on special blood and blood magic. That's all I know."

"Where did he get the blood?" Kala's suspicion rose. "Carl?"

James nodded. Kala stood and grabbed James' arm, pulling him with her. Daniel followed behind. They ran until they found Selemati and Mordami.

Without worrying about proprieties, Kala said, "We need to talk, now please."

They both bowed and followed Kala into the forest, far enough away that no one could hear what she said. She looked at both men and truly saw them for the first time. They were around the same age and looked alike, possibly they were twins. Mordami's skin grayed like he was sick and Selemati's skin showed him as all but dead, skin scaled around his cheeks and brow, and on the bridge of his nose. They had the same color eyes but Selemati's glowed in a way that made Kala's stomach curl. He was changing, somehow. They both were.

"Daddy told me you were the one who created the mutation. Why?"

"I will tell you, but you must sit with me for a while." He snapped his fingers and cups of water appeared from nowhere. "Whatever that bomb was, it's affecting me in a way I could never have dreamed."

"How so?" Daniel asked, stroking the hilt of his ax in a way that showed pride in his work. Kala was proud of it too.

"My magic is coming back. The mutation takes away magic ability, except for blood magic. Very few have resisted the mutation, and even then, not for long. Daniel was the first to fully resist it."

He paused, flexed his fingers, and sighed. "When I made it, I was under duress and compulsion. I was a respected blood specialist in Khooreja and would travel to see the sick, bringing blood with me and a spell that would reduce graft versus host. The antigens would not be exact, but they would allow the person to live and still perform magic.

"Mordami took care of my wife and children when I was away, and it was while I was away that I was captured." He shook his head and sighed again. "My wife and children were either killed or taken into captivity; I was never sure which. Carl found me one day when I returned to Khooreja, unaware of what had occurred. He told me he was a tutor, but I saw into his blood. It was tainted by power and cruelty. He had altered himself to never feel empathy toward himself or others, and never to hesitate to do what he felt he had to do. I tried to run but his henchmen caught me. They took me to Terois Manor, where they chained me in the basement lab, telling me they would kill my family if I did not do what they said. My will gave out within a month." Shame showed in his eyes and his tears fell.

"He said he had taken the blood in a land of snow, when the woman was exhausted and had nowhere to turn. He used

Many others were in the same situation. The Qazanat had destroyed what hope many people had. If the enemy succeeded, there would be more prison camps, more leaders to be destroyed, more castles conquered. How could they achieve that with so few people? People who did not work as a complete team.

"Daniel," he whispered, careful not to be overheard. "What can we do to help Kala? I haven't spent as much time with her since she became an adult, so you may know better."

"It's something she must do herself, but I have an idea. You told me you can help someone find their direction? And I can provide peace."

James nodded. "Let's do that. I can't bear to see her like this."

James cracked his knuckles and his neck then shrugged his shoulders. He tapped his legs like he was typing with one finger then rolled his hands in a downward U-shape. He stopped walking for a split-second, a side effect of his directional magic. He would lose his way for a day if he performed too much.

When he looked over, Daniel was finishing his move, an almost invisible conductor's movement with his finger.

Kala stood up straighter after they had finished and looked back at them. She gave them a mock evil eye and winked at Daniel, lighter now in her step. She stopped and waited until they leveled up with her.

"I don't know what you did, but I wish I could do it for you. Carl's nagging has stopped for now. I do have a way to repay you though." She put her hand on each of their shoulders and breathed, walking with her eyes closed. James felt his skin prickle and his muscles relax. It felt as if his bones were stretched out, and reminded him of relaxing on the beaches of the Kwajalein Islands, the sun and breeze in his hair. "I hope that works."

She grabbed their hands and walked with a smile on her face, though she couldn't hide the sadness that was underneath. This was only a band-aid. The real test would come later.

Aside from a few calluses she'd gained during the farming years and military service, her hands were smooth. Her nails needed to be trimmed and filed; she had picked at them until they were jagged. James remembered how she used to bite her fingernails; he supposed picking was a step up.

As they walked, he felt different. His Qurban strength had felt like a weight pulling him down, but he was lighter on his feet. He didn't feel weaker, he felt stronger. Though he was almost invulnerable, he had felt like he wasn't whole. Now it felt as though his heart had cleared all the muck and his lungs could put oxygen into his brain, which the mutation had rendered almost useless for judgment and seeing reality. His skin discoloration, the gray scaling and deadened look, turned a normal pinkish tan from his years in the sun, though it was a pale tan as he and Kala had light coloring from their Norwegian, Scottish, Irish, and German ancestors.

He looked over at Daniel and watched as Daniel rubbed his back, his eyes almost bulged out of his head. "Kala, thank you. My back has not felt this good since before my injury in the Marines. It's not fixed, but it feels better."

"That's good, I'm glad. Both of your... spells on me gave me an idea. I hadn't been able to help pain issues before, but I figured it out. If the nerves are what's causing that pain, ask the nerves to calm down so the vertebrae can repair. I'm hoping it does repair, because I have a feeling we will be in this fight for a long time."

James felt sympathy for Kala; he saw her look at Gul, who led them, as though she was fighting a losing battle. "Gul's lost hope yet she tries to pretend she hasn't," James said.

compel, is it so hard to compel them to be good? No, that won't work. I gotta…" She walked off.

"That daughter of yours is unsettled." Gul said, rubbing her temples as though she had a migraine.

"Unsettling, more like it," a soldier added as he watched her.

James shook his head at Daniel, who glared towards the soldier like he wanted to strangle him. Daniel stalked after Kala, looking back after every few steps to make sure he wasn't followed.

When they were gone, James asked Gul, "Can we speak in private?"

Gul nodded and led the way. "What was that? I wanted everyone to die, I wanted to be the best and strongest, yet that is not my true nature. How could a trinket do this to a person, to a company? Why were you not affected?" Gul looked at James as though he had the answers, yet he felt he could not provide them.

"All I know, my friend, is Kala seems to be a target. The way you looked at her when she approached, before the effects of the compulsion wore off, you appeared to want to change her into your image. I saw your goal, Gul, but not your motive. Because you had none. You did nothing wrong, and it was luck that kept you from hurting anyone. We both know you are the strongest in the realm. Maybe that's why you were affected the most?"

Gul smiled at his answer and patted him on the shoulder as though she feared harming him. He returned her pat by taking her hand and kissing it.

"You are a good friend, James of Earth. How do you remain so forgiving?"

"It used to be different. I was prone to anger when someone offended me, when someone tried to get to my daughters or my sons. It was tiring. And I had no power. After we met, and I learned about what I am, I saw things in a different light. I had started seeing, as a Christian, the power that love gave. How suffering doesn't mean giving up or hating others. I forgave, and forgiveness allowed me to truly love the world—well, worlds. Seeing how Kala turned out, the way she wants to help instead of harm, that increases my forgiveness because I believe she can help change the world."

"You have a lot of faith in her." Gul's smile brightened.

"Of course. She's my daughter." They chatted a little more about Kala. About Daniel. About their chances, and they did not stop until Kala approached. She was holding a bagful of those trinkets and an injured squirrel.

Kala cried while looking at the squirrel. "Daddy, I found her next to these. I couldn't leave her there, she's so sweet even while she's hurt."

"Bring her here," James said, motioning to a clearing nearby. "Give me the bag. Okay, be calm, Kalabear. You can do this. Remember how you healed our wounds? Do the same to this creature."

Kala took a deep, shaky breath and placed the squirrel on the ground. It wriggled out of her hands and stood instead of lying down, its tail quivering with pain and fear. James watched as she caressed the squirrel, starting with its head and using both hands to massage its ears. The squirrel's tail stopped quivering and curled into its natural position. She moved down its neck and the squirrel leaned into her hand then leaned into the other. When her hand moved to its shoulders, she paused and loosened her grip, trying not to injure the squirrel further.

as Gul looked at her with more interest. Her toes tapped in agitation. "What is it?" Kala asked, rougher than she intended.

"You are strange, unpredictable, yet you put your heart and soul into everything you do. Why is that?"

"I don't know; it's how I've always been. I didn't like war, yet I fought in wars… well, from the skies. I don't like chores, yet when I do them I obsess over perfection. Perfection never comes, and never will come, so I've accepted that I must do what I must do, and I get joy from helping others. And being seen for who I am, not what others want me to be."

"I have never seen a person who accepts flaws the way you seem to. For myself, I cannot stand them, nor shall I ever. I will be strong and must be strong. If I fail, others will suffer." She looked askance at Kala. "Can you heal people the way you healed those animals?"

"Yes, I can. With difficulty. The deeper the wound, the more I feel and absorb their wounds. That is why I fainted while healing Moonshine."

"Who is Moonshine?" Gul's voice shook and was lower than it had a few minutes before. She appeared suspicious.

"The majestic horse."

"Why harm yourself for the sake of an animal?" Her voice was inquisitive, not hostile, so Kala answered, though part of her still wished to walk away, to be by herself. Carl was back, saying the same thing in her head, and the other spirits hid from the fires in front of her.

"They are better than us. Pure. They do not hunt for greed, only for food. They do not take over nations and make arbitrary rules that only benefit a few, leaving the rest of us bereft and broken. They aim to help, to love, to be loved. You can see, just the way these two animals treat Daniel and me." She looked over at Daniel. The squirrel was now in his lap, eating an almond and enjoying the fire.

Gul watched the animals for some time then stood and asked Kala to join her. She led them to the clearing with the animals and said, "I will open your strength center for this task and the tasks to come. You will not need this again." She pointed at the remaining animals. "These were injured with weapons, not magic. They will be easier on you. Still, do not overwork yourself. We pin our hopes on you."

Kala could not tell if Gul was mocking or serious, but either way, too much was on the line and she could not know how to keep that hope going. How could she when she had no clue what they faced, ever? Still, she was willing to try. Kala nodded towards Gul, then Gul placed her hand on Kala's back, right behind her heart, and tapped her fingers three times. Kala's nerves fired; she could feel her own body healing more than it had before. Her wounds appeared to close, and she felt alive for the first time since they were captured. Her breath deepened on its own; she breathed in so deep she felt she would fly away with the clouds. She was glad concentration was not needed for her lungs to activate this time. It was hard to focus on tasks when she held her breath, a habit her brain had formed during times of struggle. "Thank you," Kala said, feeling the effects of Gul's fingers even more as time passed.

"You are most welcome. Use it wisely." She stepped aside, urging Kala to move closer.

Two other horses, several bunnies, and even dogs, lay in the clearing. She moved to the horses first, knowing they would take more energy. She didn't want to exhaust herself and be unable to help them. A gray mare with silver mane and tail had a side wound. It looked like a spear wound and it had a taint of magic on it. The weapons must have been dipped in a poison that made its victims feeble. The horse would not have been on its side lying so passively had it not been poisoned. She laid her hands on it and healed it faster than she expected. During the task, her mind swam for a moment, but she did not feel as though she took on all the horse's pain this time, even though she could feel it.

Feeling confident, she moved to the next horse, a chestnut mare with a sun on its forehead and white socks. It reminded her of her mother's Arabian mare, who she rode often when she was young. She placed her hands on the horse and it stood up, whinnying and shaking its head. When Kala stood, the horse bowed to her. She scratched its head between its ears and moved on. The horse moved to let her pass. The dogs were next; they looked like a black lab and a golden pit bull, both with pointy ears pulled back. She attempted to heal them both at once and was surprised when it worked. Her brain jolted when they were healed. Daniel came running into the clearing, Nutter on his head and Moonshine trotting behind.

"I felt something strange just now. What happened?" He was panting like he had sprinted, something he hated doing.

Kala stumbled as she moved, her head floating and spinning. "Doggies, healed. Lightning bolts in my brain."

Daniel walked up to her and to the dogs. He petted the golden one on the head and the black one nudged him, forcing him to pay attention to her. "They're perfect. This one is Lana." He looked confused when he said it.

"This one is Starling," Kala said, petting the golden pit on the head. Starling licked Kala in the face and ran circles around her. "I need to get the others." She pointed at the bunnies. She questioned how she knew what to call the dog, and how Daniel appeared to know his dog's name.

Starling followed her over to the bunnies, looking at them as if they were toys to play with. Kala said, "Not for puppies," and picked up the bundle of bunnies. She cuddled them until they moved. Her dizziness increased, but she felt a sense of accomplishment. The bunnies hopped around the forest, nibbling on fallen leaves. Kala felt better but sleepy. "We can name the bunnies later since there are five of them. I need to rest now." Daniel took her hand and led her to their sleep spot.

"No one will bother you. Sleep now, we are safe."

James lay on one side, Daniel on the other, Lana and Starling squeezed between them. Starling burrowed under Kala's blanket, between Kala and her father. The squirrel settled on Kala's stomach and the horses gathered around, two of them nameless. The bunnies huddled between the horses and them. No one approached their sleep site, and Kala slept more deeply than she had in a long time. No nightmares, just peaceful dreams of healing all those on their side, even those trapped in Terois Manor.

The next morning, something hitting her in the gut woke her from her healing sleep. She grabbed her stomach and curled up. When another foot came down, she rolled out of the way and kicked the foot right as it hit the ground. The culprit fell, and Kala seized the moment to take her dagger, which appeared in her hand on her command, to the man's throat. He looked familiar, and realization dawned on her. "You're one of Gul's men."

His mouth foamed like a rabid animal. Sweat dripped from his brow and his skin greyed in the morning sun. She put one hand on his chest, trying to feel what ailed him, and found it. A seed of the Qurban mutation. Could that be why the figurines littered the

"You are a walking marvel," he said, half to himself. Kala couldn't say whether that was a compliment or an insult, but she let it slide. He moved closer to her, as did the other Qurban, but she wondered if it was her imagination. She could be having paranoia issues, but could anyone blame her?

"How was the mutation created?" she asked, hoping to get things back on track. She hated having attention. Even now, she wanted to walk into the forest and never come back, be away from everyone except her father and her love. But she had to stay, be an adult, face the danger instead of fleeing or freezing in her skin.

Mordami looked towards Gul, hesitating. Guessing the cause of his hesitation, Kala nodded to urge him to speak. "It began with the herbicide concoction, Agent Orange, created by the Qazanat and put into the hands of those who wished to use it. Then Carl found the cursed arachnid, the tick, which became his favorite pet; he infused ticks with the mutation, which contained Agent Orange, the venom of a lionfish, and Kala's blood. He tested animals, people, even fish, trying to find the bloodline that was foretold to thwart him. The day he began at Terois Manor was the day he learned who would come to defeat him.

"He could not believe a woman could win against him, as puny and unfit as the Qazanat believed women were, yet he was scared. Any who questioned his courage disappeared. Carl had the power of compulsion as well as expulsion. He could compel a person for an extended period and only release them when their usefulness had expired. He also expels people's memories from when they were themselves."

"What did he do at Terois Manor?" Daniel gripped his knees. *Could he cut off his circulation that way?* She looked back at Mordami. He appeared just as bothered. She felt strange, as if nothing surprised her, and she just wanted Carl gone from her life. No obsession, no emotion, just... exhaustion?

"He mentored Terois Manor's eldest son, its heir, Amell Terois. The boy needed a powerful mentor, and no one suspected Carl performed blood magic. He was reported to be the greatest non-guardian sorcerer in Abeja, and no great sorcerer would dare dabble in blood magic." Mordami scoffed. "Blood magic was not the problem; the man was. He compelled Amell to kill his brother and sister in cold blood; instead, Amell ran away to another land. He has not been seen since. His parents... " Mordami shuddered. "His father is Qurban and his mother is used as a breeding mare in Ahteja, where her powers deplete over time. But that is for later. Carl held them in the dungeons until his research was complete, then he took off, leaving the manor empty, save those in the dungeons. He returned two weeks later and half had died, including the children. He threw their bodies into the ocean."

Mordami paced, coming far closer to Kala than the other three. She inched away, not being rude but needing her bubble space. "He somehow found pieces of prophecy, which he forced me to translate; he knew he must go to Earth and find James Skaggs. I do not know what he did while he was there; I know he used Kala's blood, and yours, James, after you had been bitten and infected by a tick." Looking at James and Kala in turn, he said, "I regret writing your name, my friend. I am afraid I started it all."

"No, Mordami," James said. "Carl started it, and, if he is somehow alive, we will finish it."

"That is another matter we must discuss." Gul was on her feet again, as if she spoke in a general counsel. "What are the chances Carl is still alive?"

He bowed his head. "One hundred percent, now that I have reconsidered. He injected himself with a potion made from Kala's blood, and Daniel's blood. He will be immune to his own creation; he will heal. We must find a way to be rid of him, once and for all."

They ate after the conversation, ravenous from exhilaration, yet no one could stomach more than a few bites. To Kala, the predicament was personal. Her existence was putting others in trouble.

The animals came back, sensing they were needed, and sat at the edge of the forest. They shied away from the new batch of Qurban recruits who ate as though they had been starved.

The new mutants stared at Kala for the entire meal. Feeding them was a chore. Neither she nor her comrades knew what they would do, and when loosed for a moment, they looked as though they would revert to violence then fawned over Kala again. She almost wished they would fight; the way they looked at her chilled her, like they would sacrifice themselves on her altar if she asked.

"I want to try something." Kala moved towards one of the untied Qurban and moved to touch him. Daniel blocked the path, and she heard a snarl behind him.

"They might hurt you." Daniel moved aside and looked at the Qurban closer. "The way he looks at you makes me nervous."

"That's why I wish to try something, anything. I want them to be people again, dammit! At least then I would have an idea of what went on in their heads."

"Let's restrain him again first." Daniel had no problem tying the Qurban again—he never looked away from Kala. She hated this mutation; these men had less will than a couch. At least a couch never had to kill for anyone. Hundreds of the men had been killed in the fight. Their bodies disappeared, but Kala felt as though each man or woman died, like a light bulb *click* as the power is switched off.

She knelt in front of the prone Qurban who tried to lower himself further to be below Kala's eyeline. Her nausea threatened to spike, and she pushed it back. Now was the time to learn what she could do for these people.

without taking love or strength of spirit into account. Simply malicious actions without motivation or intent. It was chaos, and fighting it took everything I had. Thanks to you two, others can be cured."

"Wow, that's the most I've ever heard you say in one sitting, Daddy." Kala laughed. "You helped to create this cure, remember? In fact, without you creating me, I would not be here to heal you."

"Wrap your head around that." James laughed and rested his hand on Kala's shoulders. "Let's help the others."

Kala and Daniel walked behind James, holding hands from time to time. Daniel's hands were sweaty from anxiety periodically on the journey. She could feel his emotions in her heart, masking her own, which were immense. They didn't know what would happen with the others. Maybe it would be the same? But Kala sensed another obstacle would arise, just like they always did. She could run over or through these obstacles, but she could not run around them or back to the beginning. None of them could go back to the beginning.

The trek was short but Kala's mind took the time to form a mountain from a molehill—her stomach churned. She felt like she swam in her own sweat. Her breathing stopped and she fell. The dagger fell out of her pocket, bounced, then landed tip-first on her arm. The blood droplet tingled as it entered her blood stream and she collapsed. "Daniel, you have to go alone with Daddy. I need a minute. Here, take this with you." She handed him the dagger.

"Are you sure you're okay?" Daniel knelt next to her and looked into her eyes. "Your pupils are dilated. What happened?"

"The dagger stabbed me, or touched me, whatever you would call it. It didn't pierce my skin, but I feel... different. I felt the antidote go into me."

"What will it do to her?" Daniel asked. He looked around. "Where is Selemati? Get him, now!"

James ran back to Selemati; he came back right away. "He's coming. He was in the middle of… something."

"Whatever it was, he'd better hurry. This is unexplored territory and Kala's tested it by accident!"

"It's okay, Daniel." Kala tried to stand, but Daniel pushed her back down. She opted to sit with her legs crossed instead. "I feel better now. Stronger, even. I feel…" She levitated, though she couldn't tell if it was real or a delusion. "Cloudy," she said. Her head was in the clouds, where she could see the land below. Free. She felt free.

Atop the cloud was a fortress. Beautiful, majestic. Shining with the sun, it appeared to be made from crystallized cloud, so was it ice? She wanted to check it out. But something pulled her back.

"Kala, Kala, can you hear me?" Selemati knelt at her side, viewing her as though she was an anomaly, not a person who had tripped. Kala looked into his eyes.

"You are not only you. You lost someone, didn't you? Your wife and children? I can… I can see them in your eyes. You had three sons, and your wife was another blood specialist. You do not know if they are dead, but you want to find them."

He stepped away from her yet still looked as if he wanted to see more. "Mordami, come," he yelled, standing a safe distance from Kala, his eyes fixed on her.

"What is it?" Mordami spoke faster than normal, like he was irritated or anxious. She hoped this new knowledge and magic would enable her to help them better.

"She… knows about Lolata and my three sons. How? Did you tell her? Or James?"

"No," Selemati blocked her. "He is not well. This man did not have what we thought. It is something new. Something… I do not know. The antidote must have reacted with it."

"If it's something different, maybe I can heal it. I can't place it, but there's something…" She closed her eyes and relied on her senses. "Something off about him."

"He has a demon inside him." Mordami approached them with an amulet. "It is as I feared, this infection is loose in the world. We are in the midst of a storm."

Kala turned away and looked to the stars. How had time passed her by?

The moon hid its face behind a cloud. *Moon, light up the night so I can see what to do.* Its lunar glow lit the ground around them and landed square on Kala's face. She felt a deep connection with the world, and she could just sing. And sing she did.

Come all ye dancers to dance in the night
Come all ye singers and sing to the fight
Dance with me and sing this ol' song
We will rejoice all the night long

She danced around the possessed man; his mouth foamed and eyes rolled as she wove past and around him. She picked up dirt from the ground and threw it above her and felt the wind in her hair as it blew the dirt away. She didn't think, she just did what felt right. Kala knew she wouldn't recall it afterwards; she never did. She could have been possessed herself.

As she danced and hummed, the man kicked and screamed, writhed on the ground. Something was happening to him, but she saw it as if through several panes of windows across her eyes.

Stressful situations were just movies of her life, and movies always had a happy ending. Or did they?

She tripped and landed on top of the bound man. His head jerked and the foam burned her skin until she wiped it off. The pain would last a while but she hoped it would heal better than some of her other wounds.

She could not stand and didn't know why. The man turned and smiled into her face. "Your fate is worse than mine, whore of the sun." He gasped, and a dark shadow flew from his eyes into the night. It veered away as it left, as though afraid of her.

The man collapsed as Daniel, James, and Gul rushed to her. Selemati saw to the man.

"What did he say to you?" Daniel asked. "I tried to get to you but there was a forcefield or something. You looked scared."

"Carl *is* alive," Kala said between sobs. Her ribs hurt; every breath was the agony of being trampled by buffalo herds... plural. Her face felt swollen and she knew she would have red splotches for days.

Daniel led her to the forest, where they could talk in private. He beckoned James over and she was grateful. The story didn't need to be told twice. When they were on the banks of the water, Starling and Lana approached, nuzzling each of the Roshanra. Animals must be immune to the mutations. James sat and pulled his legs close to his body, away from the water. "What is it, my Kalabear?"

"You said Carl is alive. How do you know? How can you be sure?" Daniel looked both angry and anxious; she felt her own anger and anxiety rise. They would often absorb each other's emotions. She didn't need that right now, but she had never mastered putting up a shield when she was around him... she cared too much.

"Yes, I'm sure. That man, he called me 'whore of the sun', then a shadow flew from him, back towards Terois Manor. I don't think that was a devil. I think it was part of Carl's soul, so black from his deeds that he can infect others with his evil."

"Why does that phrase tell you all this?"

"It's time I told you what happened while he held me captive."

26

Kala stood and paced, wanting to vomit out the memories so she could move on. "I don't mean to dump this on you, but I need to tell you why I did what I did. You already know he raped me..." She caught her breath. "God, I hate that word. But it's the easiest way to describe it. He didn't stop there. He forced some of the Qurban to do it... He threatened to have you do it, Daddy." She couldn't handle her emotions; she let her brain do what it needed to survive. *Don't fight the dissociation, just continue with your story.*

"While I was in there, the first day, multiple men forced themselves on me, not caring how much they hurt me. They appeared to enjoy my pain. I was bruised, swollen, bleeding every day. When they learned I could heal overnight, they intensified their attacks... put sharp objects inside of me. One thing they forced inside me was barely smaller than a baseball bat; it broke my pubic bone. My wounds might have healed, but the pains remained. I still have them." She stopped.

It was a castle, constructed from dark tar and stone, stark against a backdrop of monstrous trees that ate each other. Their sighs, groans, and belches filled the air like the sound of volcanic mud. No animals' cries and snuffling split the night, only those from the monsters in the water. Something pulled her toward the castle; she wanted to explore. She needed answers, and her questions shouted across her and over each other, driving her to insanity. She would never learn all she should about this Qazanat world if she kept fretting about everything.

"What happens if we get caught here?" She tried to appear calm, crossing her hands in front of her, interlocking her fingers as she stretched her back muscles. Her rhomboid muscles were sorest from the constant tension. She wiggled her jaw, realized she had been clenching her teeth.

"Our souls will be trapped here. I will not be reborn, and you will be nothing more than another body on Derowa."

"Did we really travel here, or are we seeing it from your memories?"

"We are betwixt the worlds."

Kala nodded. She thought she understood what Shenala meant. She felt as if she lived between worlds all the time. It was like looking through a pane that would not give her a full understanding of the world. "Let's go inside. The... castle... seems abandoned...?" *The whole world felt abandoned.* "We may get lucky and not run into anyone."

Shenala looked sideways at Kala and sighed. Perhaps it was a habit? She put it out of her mind as soon as Shenala agreed. "Touch nothing. I do not know what would happen should we touch a cursed item."

Kala understood, and she looked for a way in. As they approached the castle, Kala noted every obstacle she would need to cross if they needed to flee. Entering the front door was out of the question. That would be asking for attention. But the structure had no windows. Did the inhabitants live in the dark? She looked to the sky and noticed there was no sun. How did they keep warm? *Focus, Kala. You'll trap yourself if you don't focus.*

"How do we get in?" Kala whispered. Her nerves took over; she connected back with her sleeping body, felt her body on Derowa turn over—its restlessness reflected to her spirit. She had to breathe, had to stop worrying and just... be... calm.

"The door ahead is our only way. A law exists here that none should lock their doors. We may pass."

Kala did her closed eye breathing ritual; she stood taller, as ready as she would ever be. For some reason Shenala moved behind Kala, so Kala was forced to lead the way. *Shouldn't a more familiar person, one who was showing her around, be in the lead?* Despite her questions, she stalked to the door. A reflex told her to knock, but that was ridiculous. She pulled her hand down to the knob and pushed. It opened wide, but nothing felt right about it. But still, the impulse to learn more kept her going. She would not rest until she had some answers. Answers about her importance and destiny. It had all felt like nonsense before.

She stepped onto a booby trap. An arrow shot through her; she didn't have time to react. Even though she was uninjured, she felt a little off. She couldn't explain it; it was a distant feeling, as if it was only part of her. The realization hit her: whatever happened to her spirit would affect her body. She would need to be more careful, would need to look at the floor, the ceiling, everything she passed.

27

D aniel woke to Kala moaning and tossing, sweating as if she had been in a sauna all night. Her blanket lay feet from her. She was pale, and he moved closer to check her forehead. Ouch! He pulled his hand away. Steam rose where he had touched her as if her skin was scorching, even with the sweat and without the blanket.

If he did not cool her down, she could die from her fever. "We move out in an hour," James said as he walked up from the main camp.

"There's a problem." Daniel attempted to remain calm while he picked Kala up. "Help me get her to the river. My back won't let me carry her the whole way."

"What happened?" James ran the last few yards and took Kala from Daniel. Holding her tight, he looked down at her as he moved towards the water.

"I don't know. I woke to her moans and groans. She even kicked me earlier this morning... I fear she's cursed."

"It may be. I don't know. Get Gul, bring her here. She could help us work out what's wrong."

Daniel nodded and ran as fast as he could. Sciatica ran down his leg, making him hobble. He wanted to scream, although he knew James would protect her. James was the only person he would trust to take care of Kala, aside from himself. He had heard stories of her youth and had seen James for himself. One lie to protect her did not change who he was.

Men and women had packed their belongings and formed into travel groups of five. The Qazanat ruled the land and groups larger than three weren't permitted. The Qazanat had recognized that three would not be able to protect themselves, so they needed to take this chance with the larger group. They waved at Daniel as he ran, perplexed.

Gul looked up as he approached, her eyes widened. "Kala's sick... we think... it may be a... a curse." He bent over to catch his breath as he spoke.

"Drat, I knew this was too good to be true." Gul put her hands on him. He felt some of his strength return, and his leg pained him less. "I will go with you. Where is she?"

Daniel told her as they walked. He wished he had a bicycle right now; it was at least half a mile away. It felt as if they walked faster than he ran—they were back to the campsite in half the time. He led her to the river where James waited.

Daniel panted and sweated. Gul appeared unaffected by the walk. She continued past Daniel into the water, where James dunked Kala, only her face showed in the water. "She's burning up," James said. "She woke up this way. The warter seems to be helping, but only if she is immersed. As soon as I bring her out, her fever spikes... It's worse than mine when I turned."

Gul gasped. She reached out to touch Kala but stopped short. "There is nothing I can do for her."

Daniel looked into her eyes and knew she was telling the truth. She would help if she could. "What's wrong with her?" He could not stop his sciatic leg from tapping as fast as it could.

"She is cursed, a spirit curse, one that tests the spirit to its last, breaking her body apart from the inside. She must fight it on her own; any outside help could kill her as she sleeps. In her dreams, the deepest parts of her mind will open. She will face everything she has ever feared and face herself. I do not know how it happened. No one crossed the barrier I created... we must have a spy among us."

"Is there anyone we can trust?" He could not think of anyone but the three of them. Gul was new to him—she could be lying.

"Only the cursed, and ourselves. Angela told me Qazanat reinforcements had arrived this morning. Our twenty against hundreds in the manor..." She sat down on the bank and looked at Kala, unfocused. "My sister will be doomed, just like the rest, if we do not save her. We need Kala. She is the key to understanding, though I do not know how. The Foreseer predicted she would come, broken and determined to be whole. She would find a way out and lead our people to freedom and safety. The Foreseer said there were two others who would guide her. That they would form a triad. If Kala dies today, our hope is lost. I fear we must postpone the rescue..." She stood and wrung the water from her wet clothing. "I will send word to my men. All able-bodied people must return to the base." She walked away without another word.

* ☾ ☼ *

Kala was trapped in nothingness. She heard voices from afar, which she recognized as her loved ones and Gul. James trusted Gul, and Kala trusted his judgment. After all, he had tried to push her onto the right paths in life and he hadn't judged her when she strayed from her own values. She knew he wouldn't judge her for anything if she learned from it and changed her ways.

A path formed ahead of her, red orange like molten lava; yellow lines crisscrossed it. She stepped on it; it was so cold it would have burned her had she been in her body. Yet there was heat in it, too—it was like the salves she had put on her muscles in the military.

She walked down the path for ages, noticing her body was flushed while she remained cool. It appeared this was the spirit world. She reminded herself to be careful.

Just off the path, a Rottweiler puppy pounced around, chasing a butterfly. It reminded her of her childhood when she watched farm animals play in nature. The puppy caught the butterfly, which exploded, showering the puppy with fire and molten rock fragments, setting light to its fur. Without thinking, Kala raced to the puppy, although he made no noise. A thought raced through her mind but she pushed it aside. She threw water at the puppy, not knowing how she did it. The water splashed her, but she continued to focus on the puppy. The fire remained and grew, forming a gigantic puppy-shaped lava monster, which laughed in her face.

"You come with me," it said as its snapping jaws reached for Kala. She tried to run but molten rock had formed around her ankles.

The monster picked her up, put her on its shoulder and into a cage that glittered and appeared to be made of blue diamonds. She

They reached her together, after almost a mile of swimming. They grabbed her on either side and swam to the nearest shore. "I thought this was a stream, but it's a river. That was a close one."

James held her tight; he shook with stress. Kala's nose bled. Daniel thought she would hemorrhage. He had a feeling James hadn't seen it because of flashbacks to his sister's death. He hadn't been able to save her, but he'd rescued her friend. Kala had told Daniel the story, how James always said, "It should have been me instead."

Daniel looked around. The forest was thicker on this side, with trees and rocks and brambles. There was barely any room to walk. They would have to carry Kala back through the forest and across the stream, not a simple task. "Moonshine," Daniel said as he stood. "I wonder if we can call the horse she bonded with."

"Great idea," James said, a half-smile, half frown on his face. "Call the horse, I have a feeling it will come to you since you're a musical man."

"Moonshine!" Daniel looked around, wondering if he was even in hearing range. "Moonshine!"

Pounding hooves, like thunder, came from within the forest. The noise became louder until they saw the large, black horse leap; it landed six inches from James' side and reached its huge head down to nuzzle Kala and James. Moonshine picked Kala up by her clothing, lifting her easily out of James' lap and setting her on its back.

Moonshine wasn't the only animal there. The other two horses, which had yet to be named, stood behind the trees. The dogs and bunnies and squirrel were also there, along with hundreds of other animals of every species and breed. They had an army of animals.

If he could wake Kala, they could train these animals to help them. It would be better than just the four of them and Gul's army. *Come on, Kala. Wake up. You can beat this.* He moved over to Kala and kissed her head. James did the same and whispered something that Daniel could not hear.

Kala stood, feeling the effects from hitting the wall on her body. She would bleed out from her nose before she could free herself. Forgetting her situation for a moment, she closed her eyes and focused on her healing energy. She could feel the connection growing and knew she was surrounded by her loved ones.

I can do it. I can free myself. I can stop bleeding and wake up. The whisper travelled along the bond; she felt herself stir enough to stop bleeding.

She turned around; the monster stared at her. "Didja break your brain? Better for me, as long as you feel pain."

Kala growled at the monster, a deep guttural growl. Her face and body burned but she raced towards the monster, fists bared, determined to break it apart if she had the stamina and strength. The ground beneath her gave way, forcing her to jump towards the solid ground ahead.

The monster grabbed her by the hair and dragged her towards a shack, which resembled the broken shed in her granny's back yard. "Stay here," the monster snarled as he plopped her into a chair beside a fireplace. A fireplace in lavaland? Another torture?

"Why do you want me?" Kala looked around to quell her fear. Her body appeared to lose energy in the spirit land.

He growled. "I do not want you. My master does. And I obey."

Maybe she could bond with it, get it to play a little. "What's your name?"

"I have no name. Doggo no gets name. Good doggo need no name."

She had a hard time understanding its logic. Not having a name, not being given a name? It was a sign of disrespect in her eyes. She couldn't see how the monster dog would benefit from not having a name. It was like being called "hey, you" by someone.

"Why am I here? Why does your master want me?"

The monster sat in front of her, its tail flopped this way and that. It cocked its head to one side. "Master says you must pay. I bring you to him. He rewards me with less whipping."

"That's awful! You shouldn't be treated that way!" Even demon spawns deserved some respect.

"How I be treated?" The dog's head lowered a little, as though he recognized the truth when he heard it.

Kala patted him on his chest; when he licked her, his warm, dry tongue felt like sandpaper. She giggled. "Doggos need to be shown love and have fun. What do you do for fun?"

"I no made for fun. Only work."

"We are going to play a game right now. Let's go outside." There were no toys outside, but Kala found the closest thing she could. A piece of lava rock. She picked it up and the dog cringed. "No, don't worry! I will not hurt you. I want you to play a game with me."

"What I do?" The dog scratched his head.

"You go after it when I throw it. Ready? Go get it!" She tossed the rock as far as she could, which wasn't far. The dog jogged to get the rock and came back, but the rock was nowhere to be found. "What happened to it?"

"I eat. Yum."

Kala laughed so hard she fell. It felt good, just for a moment. She felt the effect of the laughter on her body; her fever lessened as she calmed her fear and anger. She would be positive, no matter what happened.

The dog stopped laughing with her and stood up straight. "Uh-oh. Master mad. Go inside." The dog, still in its monster form, picked her up and flung her through the shack door.

Kala had only been inside for a second before a whooshing came from the fireplace. The flames danced, lamps flickered, and dust she hadn't noticed before flew, gathering into a whirlwind. A black cloud floated through the flames and formed next to Kala a full-fledged man. She did not know him but she had a feeling he knew her. "You are the one causing all these problems?"

"What problems?" Kala's brow furrowed; she cocked her head to the side.

"The rapes and torture, the starvation and decay in Derowa."

"What? Who are you to accuse me of being the cause? I did nothing to deserve my treatment on Derowa, and people keep telling me it's all my fault." *Breathe, Kala. Breathe.*

"It is your fault." The man disappeared. She looked around and found no trace of the dog.

How could it be my fault? She could find no answer. She smiled. She was finally free from the shame others had put on her!

She had *an* answer they might have given. She was born, she hadn't died, and despite everything she kept surviving. She didn't know why she kept having to go through this torture, but she had to find a way to stop it. No one else needed to feel this pain and confusion. The only way she could change it was to find a way back to her body and defeat the Qazanat. But how?

She walked around the shack's perimeter, noting how the wall rose. She spotted a crag in the rock wall and stuck her hand in the

the prison, to the entry point which was now feet away from the cabin. *Magic is neat.*

"I shall go with you. After all, it is my fault."

"You put the arrow in his home, not mine. It was not intentional, unless you're really good." She shook herself like a wet dog. "Okay, I'm ready. And I recommend you steer clear of Daddy and Daniel. They may not be as forgiving, if I'm right about what they have gone through." With this warning, they were off.

Daniel, James, the animals, and Kala's body—carried on Moonshine's back—arrived at the campsite. James watched Gul as she came to meet them. She was as beautiful as ever. He had never been with her, had never wanted to be with her, but he could still admire her beauty. They had a friendship almost as powerful as his and Marnie's, but he would never betray Marnie more than he had already when faking his death. He wasn't dead, so death did not part them. But would she forgive his lies?

Kala had not moved since the nosebleed. Daniel said the bleeding had stopped on its own. James thought that was Kala's power. She could heal anything she put her mind to, even if she was cursed. He worried for her; no one could escape a death curse.

He hailed Gul to them, and she came with a walk more graceful than the horses behind him. "How is she?" Gul asked. James saw the calm she wore to hide her fear and sadness. He knew she refused to show her weaknesses, for she saw weakness in every other part of life. Weakness in people. She had talked to him of it at length; she still saw no weakness in Kala, even while she was unconscious. Angela had told her Kala's caring nature was her greatest strength, and he knew Gul didn't doubt this.

"She is still unconscious. The warter took her away when she had a seizure, but we swam and caught her. We called to Moonshine and the animals came. They brought us back."

"Good. Is her fever gone?"

James hopped from his horse and felt Kala's forehead with the back of his hand. "It isn't gone, but it has gone down."

"I thought as much. She is returning."

"How can you be sure?" Daniel leapt from his horse; he approached Gul, anger in his eyes. "You haven't even looked at her. How do you know?"

"Because he has her." Gul nodded her head towards Kala. Daniel turned and saw a man who walked towards them.

"Loami! Where did you come from? What is the meaning of this?" James ran to meet him.

"You know him, James?" Daniel stayed with Kala's body. "Loami, you said? Why does that sound familiar?"

"He is the King of Lusterio. The fountain you seek is there." Gul approached until she stood behind James.

"Why are you here?" James walked up to the man with anger in his heart, and suspicion too. From the corner of his eyes, he noticed that Daniel's fists were clenched, ready to fight if necessary. "What did Gul mean, you have Kala?"

Kala stirred on Moonshine, and Moonshine sensed the movement and tip-tapped on the spot, eager for her to rise. "I brought her back." Daniel moved towards him and Loami put up his hands. "It was a mistake. Kala can vouch for me, I swear. I put a trap in the Arresto castle on Tarekana. She found her way there... somehow. Her spirit entered and was hit with the cursed arrow I placed as a booby trap." Daniel growled at the same time as James did, and Loami added, "It was meant for Carl!"

Kala sat up and slid off Moonshine, holding onto his mane as though it was rope. Her eyes were glazed but James could see her coming back. "He's telling the truth." Her body wavered as she spoke, and Daniel rushed to her. "He released me as soon as he recognized I wasn't a bad guy. An innocent mistake." She wilted, landing soft on the ground as though she had a pillow to break her fall. A pillow of shadow.

"What is that power?" Gul asked. "Where did you learn it? I thought you were a water creature."

Loami smirked. "Is it too close to air for you, Gul? I learned it on my own… when I thought Carl was coming after me. I needed to hide. I was right. He killed my parents, after he killed my brother and sister. He tried to turn me to his cause, wanted me to think I had killed my siblings, and that my parents killed themselves out of grief. I know the truth, and he will pay."

"Everyone wants him to pay," Daniel said, looking angrier than he had in a while.

"Not everyone," Loami said. "She wants to heal him." He pointed at Kala.

"She was serious with that?" Gul asked. "I thought she was brainstorming. But it makes sense. This fighting violence with violence is nonsense, never-ending. We must end it somehow or the world will end."

"Worlds," Daniel added.

"Valid point," Loami said. "She should be as good as new any moment. I am sorry for the hassle." He looked to all of them. "May I stay and join the fight? I am tired of hiding. I will use my sneaking and poisoned arrows for good."

"Sure." Daniel was the first to speak. "Just don't touch Kala again."

"I won't. I am not interested in her, by the by. I love my wife."

James understood the sentiment but it appeared Daniel did not. He watched Loami like a hawk, even asking him questions about his history. One question Daniel wanted answered was how Carl had gotten close enough to him and his family to kill them all. "I will answer your question once Kala is awake and focused. She deserves to know as much as you."

"How do you know so much about us?" Daniel sounded calmer but the throbbing vein in his forehead betrayed his anger.

"My wife is Naomi Moredock."

"The Foreseer," Gul said. "She is the one who told me I needed to get James to Derowa to save our world. I did not know what that meant at first, but then I saw. He was the first mutation."

"What?" Kala sat up, shaking her head. "Did you say he was the first mutation? How did the Qazanat get my blood?"

James moved towards Kala. "How are you, Kala? Remember, you know how it happened. The ticks transmitted part of the curse, and Carl had taken your blood when he hurt you."

Kala shook her head like she had when she was confused as a child. "I found some notebooks in Tarekana. They should be in my bag. Can someone fetch them?"

"I'll get it," Daniel responded, although he looked as if he wanted to hold Kala instead.

Kala stood up to follow him. When James moved to help her, she said, "No, Daddy. I can do it. But please come with me." She looked at Gul and Loami. "Please, wait here. We just need a moment."

James smiled, proud of his daughter, and worried as well. She was behaving different to normal. She appeared vacant. What was going on in her head?

28

Kala was tired of being chased, of fighting and being chased some more. Captured at every turn. She was gullible and caring when she needed to be ruthless and caring from a distance. The spirit entrapment was the last straw.

Once they freed everyone from the Qazanat dictatorship, she would go on her enlightenment journey. She would find the strength she needed. She knew she would never finish her quest alive if she didn't evolve, and neither would anyone else. *Focus, I need focus. Breathe. That's it, just breathe. Everything will be okay if I breathe.*

"Kala, what's going on? Are you hurt? Did that bastard hurt you?" Daniel's arm waved; he pointed between Loami and her. She guessed what he was insinuating.

She took his hand. "No, he didn't hurt me. The arrow wasn't meant for me, and as soon as he realized I wasn't a Qazanat leader, he released me."

"Release you?" James moved in closer.

Kala told them about the place where the curse had sent her. They waited to ask questions until the end; lights shone in their eyes at the end.

"You mean there's a place we could send Carl where he would have to face what he had done and would not be released until he repented?" The way James worded it, Kala thought of a Biblical hell. Well, the place *was* surrounded by lava.

"Yes, that's the curse that Loami created. But I think there needs to be a push. Some spell or curse that forces Carl to feel empathy. Because no matter how much facing he does, he won't change without empathy."

There was a short, quiet moment. Kala took advantage of it; she hugged James then hugged and kissed Daniel. James looked away, for which she was grateful. She didn't want to stop kissing Daniel. His breath was her breath, his heartbeat her own. Her head swam in delight and cried out for more of the love she felt with him.

A piece of her healed as they bonded, soul to soul, until they needed to come up for air. She was a little unsteady on her feet but still attempted to boop him on the nose. A boop he evaded and gave back. She laughed, which brought a smile to his face. "It's good to hear you laugh again. I've missed you so much. I will never forgive that bastard."

"That's just it," Kala said. "We have to forgive him to move on. I've been holding in my anger and it's haunted me. When I let go of the anger, I'm me again. And I must forgive to survive. Otherwise it will eat me from the inside." She pulled out the notebooks. "And I think these," she tapped the notebooks, "may tell us that that was their goal. It's a feeling I have."

"What is in the notebooks?" Daniel took his; it was torn in places. Kala thought Carl would have a harder time pinning down

Daniel. He was a complicated man at times, and more loving than he let on. Chills overtook Kala, much like they used to, running down her spine and giving her stamina for the day. Happy chills. She shook her head to get back to the moment.

"Right, the notebooks... Sorry, I was distracted." Daniel laughed, James smiled and nodded. "They seem to be about us. They each have our names on them..." She paused. "We need to include the others. They could come in handy, and they know more about our proposed fates than we do. Maybe they can help us decipher the details. I didn't get a chance to peruse them, so I'm not sure what's in them."

"Should we read them before we ask?" James looked down at his. "What if there are personal things we would rather others did not know about us?"

"Good point, Daddy, but let's read them quick. We need to get on with our journey. Something ominous in the air pulls me to rescue the captives." They quieted then read their own notebooks. Kala's started with a curse on the obstetrician. "Haha, beat you from birth, it seems."

Daniel looked up from his reading. "What?"

"The Arrestos are the reason why the obstetrician delivered me early, according to this. I think we'll find plenty of attempted thwarts as we read through."

"That makes sense," James said with tears in his eyes. "Someone pulled my sister down, in the warter. That is why I couldn't save her."

This time, Kala didn't giggle at his pronunciation of water. She felt his pain, and shame, and imagined taking some of it so he didn't have to bear it alone. She always knew that he had a hard time with it, but the pain was fresh, the wound torn open, flowing out as though it needed to purge. She would help him purge, but she had to help herself. She couldn't forget that he was her father, not a part of her.

Daniel said nothing as he read, though his ears could have steamed from the amount of anger he showed. He was the opposite of her, needing to discover information on his own before explaining his life. She could respect that; it was one of the things she admired about him.

Every thwarted scheme was the same. She had managed to thwart the threats to her life without knowing, and that's why he had begun taking things into his own hands. She read that he had influences with certain people. People who had forced themselves into her life. After this she had been controlled and pushed around. But she overcame that and met Daniel. All those moments had led to this one. The asshat's plans had unintended results: she had become stronger each time she had disrupted their plans.

They passed around the notebooks. Every one of them was the same. With Kala, they had tried to force her to be submissive to their way of thinking. With James, they had mutated him and left him with his family, hoping he would harm or kill Kala and be unable to live with himself. That's where Gul had come in, and then there was no more information about him until he was captured with Angela and Sammi. "There's a note—I think Carl must have a notebook on every powerful foe."

Daniel's was a different story. They had kidnapped him as a child, before he was old enough to know anything of his family or himself. They had tried to curse him, but he had found a guitar and once he began playing, the curse melted away like ice turned to water. He had continued teaching himself to play, not just one but several instruments.

Kala had a theory that music was as much a part of him as his eyeballs, and he would take care of his music as much, if not more, than his eyeballs. His love of music would save him.

"I'm ready, are you?" Kala asked when they returned to the others. "We have to move. Soon. Tonight or tomorrow morning at the latest."

"What's the hurry?" Loami asked, prompting the others to wonder as well.

"Before I woke, I had a dream. The captives... they are turning... somehow, into something different... less than human. There's so much hatred in the air, and they want nothing more than death and destruction. I have a *feeling* that, once they are changed, they will be released from the manor."

"Well, that is what we want," Gul responded before it dawned on her. "With the mutation? They are some of the most powerful Derowans. The damage they will cause will be monstrous!"

"That's right. So, let's get going. None of this is useful to you right now... but I think it could be useful to us."

"I don't understand it either. But we will learn at some point," James added. "Our story doesn't end tonight."

They raced to the Manor, though they were forced to go the long way around. Kala was not bogged down by hatred or fear or shame or grief, so she moved lightly. She finally believed she could do anything she put her mind to. Anything was within the realm of possibility. And right now rescuing the captives was within the realm of possibilities.

The back gate was locked but Loami appeared to know a lot about the manor; he let them in. Kala even thought she saw a key summoned into his hand. They walked past seashells and coral gardens which surrounded a fountain of daggers, into the area where she had fallen the last time she was there. It was strange how much more she saw this time around. There was clarity, as if the panes had been removed from her eyes.

When they stuffed themselves in the small opening, which appeared to be a mausoleum, Loami stood back and indicated that Kala and Daniel and James gather around.

"These are the evolution keys. Only the Roshanra can use them. They only work when you are ready. Do not lose these."

"Why are you giving them to us now?" Kala looked at the silver skeleton key; she longed to touch it.

"We do not know if we will be dead or alive when this is over." With that, he walked towards a wall paneling and tapped it once. It shook. A small staircase appeared.

"You'll have to tell us how you know everything," Daniel said, still seeming unsettled by this new addition to their group.

Nonetheless they each took a key, feeling the energies of each key before selecting. Perhaps they were linked to each Roshanra?

The staircase opened onto a junction where the dungeon met the lab. Kala shivered and rubbed her arms, looking over at Daniel and James. She regretted her decision to go along with unseen plans, but she no longer blamed herself. Loami's curse had reenforced her confidence.

"Gul, is that you?" Angela must have felt her sister's aura. Gul moved towards the cell.

"Be careful," Kala said. "It may be a trick."

"Angela, I have been so worried since you stopped..." Gul fell silent.

Kala moved forward and saw what Gul saw. Angela stood there, holding her own heart in her hand. It was still partially connected but she had ripped it from her chest. Blood saturated her body and pooled below her in the water, not blending in, separate, as though the water feared her blood.

"I will not open that door," Loami called, standing on the other side of the hallway, looking in at Angela.

"I may be able to help," Kala said. She rolled up her sleeves and knelt, placing her hands in the water. *Sahata sahaty bala wa beyon*, she chanted, not knowing if it meant anything—she performed better if she spoke the words that came to her. A blue light emitted from her; it traveled the length of the water, into the cell and beyond.

"A light's surrounding her," James called. "I think it's working."

Kala continued her chant, careful not to share anything of herself but to use the water to heal. She would be useless if she used her own energy to heal everyone.

The healing took an eternity, so when she felt it was complete, she stopped and stood. Looking up from where she knelt in the water, she saw Angela standing whole once more with a strange, foreign look in her eyes. She looked at the other prisoners—Grace, Sammi, and many others—all of whom had the same foreign look in their eyes. "We won't free them from the cells just yet. Something is off. I think they are being remote controlled. If we free them, we could find ourselves in a pickle." Kala stopped. Her stomach growled. "Pickles sound good right about now. I'm famished…"

"It's about time you eat." Daniel smiled at her as James sighed in relief.

"You didn't eat after you woke," Loami said as he looked her over. "No, no, no…" He paced back and forth, splashing in the water. "Wait here, I'll get you something from the kitchens."

"Make sure it's not poisoned or anything," she said. He looked back. "Loami, I spent half my time here clearing potions from food before I would let people eat it. All without making a noise or movement. It was exhausting."

"You're impressive," he said, then ran off into the shadows.

Daniel pulled her around the corner. He looked serious, and she could imagine why. "Kala, you've regained your appetite! That's great!" He booped her on the nose, then an uneasy look crossed his face. "Wait, why did he call you impressive?"

"I don't know." Kala had a hard time figuring out why anyone thought positive things about her sometimes. She had stopped questioning people's motives and now just watched out for clues of intent.

"Nothing... happened with him, did it?"

"I don't even know him. What is going on? Are you well? You have a fervent look in your eyes, and I've never seen that..." She reached to touch his forehead. He flinched but she could feel a fever. "Please, let me try to heal you. You have a fever."

He took a step back, breathed, then came back. "You're right. I feel... paranoid. Like everyone is out to get me. I can't control it."

"Here, I have an idea. Link yourself with me. Our strengths will enhance and maybe you can see how I think."

Daniel hesitated but Kala took his hand. She imagined her spirit holding hands with his.

Everyone's looking, they're gonna know. Oh no, nothing works, nothing will work out.

Hey, Daniel. He jumped. *Why don't you try your music magic? That will help us all, and you will see that we will succeed, even if it is just a little.*

How are you so positive right now?

I just have this… feeling. I feel things, and it's amazing and wonderful and I want to share it.

Loami came back with an apple and some cheese for each of them. "We will all need our strength."

I agree with you, Daniel. There is something… off about him. He's hiding something, and I wish I knew what it was so I could chillax.

Okay, so maybe I'm not completely paranoid. They continued to hold hands as Daniel handed Kala his apple. She gave him the cheese before he gave her some back. *Two apples are not enough for you. I wish we could have a feast. Are you strong enough?*

Kala flexed her biceps. *What do you think?* They both laughed and everyone looked at them.

"We were hangry, now we're all better," she said, trying to get them to look away, but they didn't.

"You linked, didn't you?" Gul looked at them with a fire in her eyes. She answered her own question. "Yes, they did. This is how we will win. James, you link with me, and Loami, you shade yourself and the others."

James looked as if he regretted not being bonded with Kala, but he accepted Gul's hand with a dutiful smile. Kala could understand his hesitation. If her theories were correct, he was attracted to Gul and had a hard time not betraying her mother. Kala knew her mother had moved on, in a way, but she had never remarried, or even dated. James, well, Kala didn't know what he had or had not done. One day she would have to ask him, but not about that. *Ick,* Kala and Daniel both shared the thought at the same time.

This linking is super personal. I can understand his hesitation. Don't worry about his motives or intent, Kala. I have spoken with him at length. He loves Marnie and has kept an eye on her from afar. He has a contact who reports to him when he can't be there. First about you, and then about Marnie, once you were out of the house.

She sighed. *Everyone spies on Kala. No big deal.* "Let's go, we have a bad guy to beat."

They made their way upstairs, Kala trying not to think and Daniel sharing his music with her, which helped empty her mind. James and Gul followed behind them, backup for the duo who had to face the trials head-on. Kala had no clue where Loami had gone. She told herself this was good. It meant his power worked and would hide him. The remainder of their Qurban army were also hidden.

No killing was the rule Kala had insisted upon; everyone had agreed. They needed answers, and they needed to remain pure. To know Carl wouldn't force them to become killers as well. Kala was almost glad Carl was still alive, although it made her stomach churn. She hoped her plan worked. Sometimes the baddies just needed a spark of inspiration.

She had an idea. *What if we focus on their brains? You cast music, I'll cast healing, and we will try to merge them in the process.*

What do you think that will do? Daniel appeared curious, not distrusting.

I don't know... increase their gray matter? Give them empathy? Open their prefrontal cortexes? It's an experiment.

An experiment in the middle of battle? Kala... Daniel sighed. *Okay, let's try it. If it doesn't work the first time, we won't do it again until we're in a safe space.*

Deal. Also, use your musical healing bomb. Daniel pulled out his ax.

Kala felt more hope than she had when they entered Terois Manor. She smiled. The smile was absorbed by her, and a glow spread around her. "What the...?"

"Oh, no…" Gul put her hand on Kala's back. The glowing halted; it did not subside nor increase. "That is what I was afraid of. Your evolution is beginning, but it's too much for you right now. Your extra strength makes you a target, and we cannot defend against Carl's whole army at once."

"Maybe I can use less than full strength."

"That will not work. We need all the strength we can get. No… We need a new plan. Let loose, take out as many as you can at once. This is a sign; you must be the one to take on Carl. Alone."

"Yes." Kala looked at the floor then at Daniel. "I've known that from the start. He's targeted me. It's time for me to target him instead. I am no longer a victim. And will never be one again, if I can help it."

Daniel gave her a nervous smile, but inside their heads he said, *Tap into your speedball rage. You will succeed.*

Sound feedback flowed into their minds, loud screeching as though an eagle had a chalkboard in its talons, scratching away as it screeched at its prey.

"Unlink! The interference is too much!" Gul dropped James' hand and held her ears. She was right. They unlinked and the screeching stopped. Kala felt alone, and she could see a sense of loss in the others, but Daniel's music remained with her. She would take comfort from it; she could always count on Daniel.

Kala's glow faded to a small, blue aura.

"Kala, do you know what you have to do?" Gul asked.

Kala could feel their nervousness as a shaking force around her aura. Her shield was up. She smiled. "Yes, I will go out first, alone. The baddies will see me and you can sneak around from the back."

"That would work, if the baddies weren't already here." Daniel pointed past Kala, forcing her to turn around.

Minutes dragged on and he had a thought. What if Carl was trying to compel her? *Speedball, it's Lucky. Do not let that bastard in. He wants to hurt you and everyone else. He cannot control a person who refuses to be controlled.*

He heard a *click* and felt a *whoosh* throughout his being. His pain was gone; he was in the moment, alert, more powerful and for some reason full of music which poured from him into the room. *Now we must bond with your father. You know what to do…*

Carl walked closer still to Kala, and still hadn't reached her father. Daniel's music soared through her mind, giving her strength. This was one of their moments. She was determined not to let Carl control her, but she feared him. Not because of what he did, but how much he enjoyed it.

Every torture had been unique, and she recalled them all. When she was hanging face-down from the ceiling, his goons had thrown fecal matter at her. When his tortures had caused her to look worse to him, he had forced her into an ice bath to perform some magic that "enhanced" her figure. The pain still radiated through her. She couldn't forget it.

Daddy, we need you. Her spirit tried to reach him, but he was further away than Daniel. Now she looked; Daniel was closer to him. *Daniel, I need you to try to bond with him. I'm too far away.*

She was concentrating on getting a message to Daniel and was shocked when Carl picked her up by the neck.

"You will pay for what you did, you bitch." Electric shocks radiated through her from his fingertips. "You will be mine, or you will die as the scum around you watch."

She breathed through the shocks, hiccupped on occasion, and wet herself. For a moment, she felt ashamed.

Focus, Daniel said into her mind. *He's not shocking you; he's making you think you're being electrocuted. He doesn't have lightning power. You do!*

Kala breathed and looked Carl in his shit-filled eyes. "I will never be yours, and you will not kill me." She put her hand on his face then closed her eyes, ignoring the shocks and the choking which he was intent on completing. She forced herself to open her healing eye, which originated near her solar plexus. She saw his brain and saw what she was looking for. His empathy and fear centers were low in gray matter. Picturing the gray matter was difficult, but she continued until those centers were half-full. She had never done this, but a dream had shown her what to do.

She drew power from the manor itself, and the manor offered up its power. Kala saw everything around her through the eyes of Terois Manor.

For some reason, the manor was following Loami's movements. His shadow form zoomed, handcuffing the guards with their own cuffs. He placed the keys in his pockets. Other shadows zoomed around doing the same thing.

Carl stepped back as Kala finished her spell. She felt more powerful than before, and with a start she realized her father was in her head. He was thinking how proud he was of his daughter and lent her the direction she needed to finish what she had started. She couldn't help smiling.

Unsure whether the spell would work, she backed up towards Daniel and James. *Hey, I can move. And no one is fighting. Should we just... tackle Carl?*

Gul appeared to realize what happened and created a cage from thin air. Carl was trapped. He cried with his head in his hands. Kala shook with rage and fear yet she had completed a spell that would heal him over time. Incarceration here would be remediation. It wasn't a case of holding one who could harm others after release. She let herself smile then turned to stare, incredulous at what she had done.

All the guards stood to the side, eyes bulging at their leader curled in a ball and crying his heart out. When they saw Kala looking at them, they took a step back, looked at one another, then bowed to Kala; some had tears in their eyes. She couldn't help but smile each time another bowed to her.

Daniel approached one of the guards, who flinched. Daniel whispered in his ear, and the man nodded his head then moved towards the front, with Daniel. Gul and her father stood on the other side of her and she smiled.

"Bring me the injured and compelled. They will need our support; I've gone through traumas multiple times in my life. I'll be around if anyone needs healing. I need some food before I can do anything."

In her mind, she said, *That spell on him… well, it left a film across my perception. His powers caused his brain to push back against my healing, and it's backlashed on me a bit.*

We'll help you keep an eye on it, James replied. Daniel agreed.

"I wish we could x-ray the compelled minds. Though without baseline images it's pointless."

"You need imaging?" A woman walked up, a sheet wrapped around her to hide her nakedness. "I do have it. I can go with you, wherever you need." Her smile wavered and Kala could see why. They had all gone through the same thing as her. The memories came back as she became aware of the pains she still bore.

Sobs erupted into howls and groans; people turned towards her as she screamed into the night. It was a dark night with a full moon she could see through the bricks made of water.

Daniel stood next to Kala as she screamed and cried, finally letting out the emotions she had held in for so long. She had had moments where some tears had fallen in the past, but she had not processed any of what she had been through. It had been the same before, when they first met. She was happy-go-lucky and energetic, charismatic to the core. Yet he had known from the start she was as broken as he was.

They had been through their healing together, therapy after therapy—even couple's therapy. Only after receiving proper care had they gotten through their issues together. Now he had no clue how to help her because he was in the mix as much as she was.

He attempted to comfort her, massaging her neck as she cried. Daniel caught her as she fainted again. This time, he could tell why. "She's exhausted… she had no time after waking from her coma, and then she performed her spell… on a whim. She had never practiced this spell before."

"Will she survive?" The imaging woman appeared interested in Kala, more interested than anyone else. Something was off about this woman.

"Yes, just leave her with me." Daniel scooped her into his arms and walked towards the stairs. "Loami, you said you know about this place. Is there a spare room where she will be safe?"

"Come with me," Loami replied and led him to a wall. A button to the left of a family portrait opened a panel and spun it around, to where the portrait hung on the inside. A four-poster bed, larger than a California king, sat against the wall. A blue canopy lined in white looked like waves over the bed; it was covered by a sea life comforter which appeared to come to life as he moved closer.

Loami moved in front of Daniel to pull back the covers, then he set her down.

"She looks at peace when she sleeps," Loami said. "But I can tell she is in the shadows more than I."

"Don't you dare look at her when I'm not here." There was still something he didn't trust about this man.

"You don't trust me, and I don't blame you. I will tell you my secret, and then maybe you will know I tell the truth. I do not want your woman. I have other reasons to be here, with Kala and with yourself, and with anyone else who will fight against the Qazanat."

Daniel's interest was piqued. If anyone would share their secret, he would have to share his; yet he didn't know if he could explain it. His childhood memories couldn't be trusted. He sat in one of the chairs and Loami sat in the other, both facing away from Kala.

Loami spoke, "My name is not Loami Moredock. It is one I invented, because of its meaning. 'I am lower than the dirt beneath the sea, from now to forever, Loami Moredock I shall be.' It was my motto when I wanted to come home. My real name is Amell Terois."

"Amell Terois?" That name rang a bell. "Of Terois Manor?"

"One and the same. I was born here; this room was my hideaway, when my parents got a new caretaker. This was the only room not found by... Carl." Loami-Amell made a gurgling scoff under his breath. "I hate that man with every fiber of my being. He was my last caretaker, my *mentor* as he called himself. He wanted me to dabble in the dark arts and, as I was a teen, I was naive. I allowed him to teach me the dark ways, and before I knew it, I was making my own spells.

"I pulled the lionfish from the waters. Our sacred creature, the emblem of our strength, and I killed it. I used a spell of my own creation. Words I will never repeat again. That night, my siblings, a brother and sister, died in their sleep. I blamed myself because I did not know what else could have done it. The next day, my parents killed themselves. A note was found; it only said, 'I know what you did'. It looked unfinished. I was too scared to think and ran away. Living in caves along the way, I found a refuge. My lovely Naomi found me and knew who I was. She asked me, 'Do you want to be someone else for a time?' How could I refuse? So I chose my name, a name which suited my deed.

"Many months ago, Naomi had a vision, a way to redeem my parents and siblings. She told me the truth; Carl had mutated my family and framed me. He has had his comeuppance. A good one, I should say. He will suffer because of his cruel nature."

Daniel didn't know what to say but he agreed. "Yeah, Kala is peculiar with her punishment, but she's turned him into a human. I don't think he was one before."

"He is an immortal, or close to. If this does not work, we will have to find a way to end him."

"Kala isn't going to take that well. And neither will I."

Loami departed, leaving Daniel alone with Kala. Memories surged; his truths all wrapped in a tight wad that would unravel over time. When it unraveled, would he begin fainting as Kala did? He moved over to her and kissed her forehead. Then he headed out into the chaos. He would protect her at all costs, even though she did not need his protection. She needed his love, which she would always have.

29

Kala rolled from side to side, unaware of her surroundings. She settled on her back and stretched out into an X in the middle of the bed. The room was dark and the bed was comfortable. It reminded her of Carl's bed, with the way it moved like soft waves, except this room was blue not red. Still, she didn't know where she was, but she knew she was alone.

She wouldn't scream if she was recaptured. They would want her to scream. To beg for her life as though she did not deserve it.

She scooted to the edge of the bed, it wobbled with each movement, until she felt she would roll back to the middle of the bed. Panic threatened her but she kicked panic away.

What had happened? Had her team won, or was she a captive again? Were the enemy using a new tactic? They had been ready to hurt her and everyone else. Her anger was back. It was secondary to her fear, but it was more powerful right now. She would get out and she would adapt better. That's it, adaptation. She could do it… she had done it so many times before.

She was off the bed. With her first step she wobbled so much she had to sit on the floor. From there, she crawled to the chair. A light sat on an end-table and she turned it on to see the room better.

The floors were soft carpet; they mimicked foaming ocean waves. The walls moved like the ocean, causing Kala's head to spin. Yet she couldn't look away. It was beautiful. When she had sailed, she would stare at the water, wishing she had that sense of calm. Calm would come before they sailed back to land. But people were on the land. Their energies would overwhelm her and she wanted nothing more than to go back to the isolation and the water. Shaking her head, she brought herself back to the moment. *I must find a way out. There, that's the only way, as a door is nowhere to be found.*

She walked to the portrait on the wall. She had seen the same one in another part of the house. She stared at the faces, noting similarities in the youngest boy and his father to someone she knew. *Who is it? Think!*

She had heard rumors of treachery here before that bastard took the manor for his own. What had happened to Carl? How was she alive? She couldn't recall any of the details of their journey to the manor and their attack on it. All her memories felt faint, as if they were dying. Something was wrong with her, and she had to find out what it was. *Something more was wrong. When is it not? God, I just wish this would end.*

The wall in front of her moved, spinning her with it, just like in movies. She was on the outside, facing the arena where group tortures and fights had been organized. She shivered and rubbed her arms, became colder by the second. Then she fell to the floor in a ball, shivering uncontrollably and violently.

"Get some help," Daniel said to someone she couldn't see or hear. "Help is on the way. It will be okay. Kala, look at me. Look at me!"

Kala listened to him and tried to do what he said, but she was stuck inside herself. She had to get herself out of this, but she still listened and tried to obey. "Daniel," she whispered, her voice harsh with dryness. "I... am... okay. I can do this... I must do this on my own. But stay with me if you can." She closed her eyes and dived deep into her issues.

What was she afraid of? Carl? No, not of the man but of his remorseless actions. Without remorse, a person will do anything and feel nothing. She had been compelled and trapped and held in a cage, covered in her own blood and urine. But she had lived through it and, by the appearance of things, she had triumphed. She stood, slowly and shakily, using the ground and Daniel's body as bolsters until she was upright. "I need some juice," she said, and Daniel led her to the kitchens.

On the way, she saw many people she recognized, but she couldn't recall who they were. That happened often, and her shame would arise. Why couldn't she remember people in the way she remembered people in her dreams? Dreams of people she needed to find. She knew it, and her dreams led her to believe she would find what she's looking for in Bareja. She had no clue what she sought, but she would know soon. She could feel it.

"What happened?" Kala asked as soon as she was able.

Daniel hesitated then answered, "You fainted again and went into a trance. You said something about backlash. Does that mean you were exposed to something?"

"I don't know. My memories are shaky again. I won't know how I've been affected until I can stand on my own feet, for sure."

She paused a moment. "Did it work? I tried to give him empathy. Did all our people survive?"

"It worked very well. Everyone else is fine. Don't worry about them."

"I want to see Carl, study how it's worked." Daniel gave her a confused look. "If it worked, I won't ever have to kill anyone who harms others. I can make them want to change and give them the means to change."

"You can't do that to everyone, Kala." She started to negate his comment but he stopped her. "It took all of your strength to fight his magic and to repair his mindset. According to Gul, he is one of their weakest soldiers, and he was only sent because his father is someone special. We also know they are planning something to change you; to change us. We can't protect ourselves if we hunt down every sociopath."

"I need a path," Kala said, looking at Daniel. "Defeating Carl was driving me. Now, I feel like I'm even more broken than I was, and a worse person for you and for myself. All I can think about is stopping the pain, making this end. I want to feel… whole again."

Daniel wrapped Kala into a hug, pulling her aside to let people pass. "I know how you feel, and I feel much the same. But, for now, get well. Once you are well, we can make plans."

They agreed, and Daniel took Kala the rest of the way to the kitchens, which were brighter and livelier than she recalled. The cook, Gretcha Solis if she recalled, sat Kala down with a hug and hair tussle, which did not bother her as much as she had thought it might. Gretcha reminded her of her grandmother, whistling while she cooked up a special meal for Kala who protested she would be fine with fruit and juice and water.

Daniel took an item from his pocket. He clicked a button and it opened to a guitar, an ax. He played, and the notes echoed through the kitchen. Steam from the kettle danced in time with the music, drifting to Kala and twirling around her head.

The kitchen staff laughed and sang along using whatever words they could think of. It went together and clashed in a glorious cacophony at the same time. Kala had fun for the first time in what felt like forever. She sat hunched over a cup of tea and felt sadness when the music ended. There would be time for music later. She had a journey to plan.

"We need to talk with Daddy after our meal," she announced as he put his guitar away.

"Yeah, we do. He went out with some people to scout yesterday and should be back tonight or tomorrow morning. We aren't expecting anything further to happen right now, but we need to know how long we can stay here."

"How long was I unconscious?"

"Four days."

"Four days? Why did that happen?"

"Because you were not strong enough for what you did," Gul said from behind them. "Be careful and learn your limits or you will have a worse fate in future. Still, we thank you for defeating this amateur. Your next foe will be far more fearsome and has more in store for you and us than we could ever imagine. We have not discovered their goal for Derowa, but we know some of their motives."

"What motive could they have for the torture and murders?"

Gul sat across from Kala and Daniel and pulled out the notebooks she had found. "These were made from human skin. I researched the Terakanans and learned they are not human. They... inhabit the bodies of people after taking their souls. They consume souls, thereby consuming the powers of that person.

They want to use your bodies and souls, because if I am correct, you two will be the most powerful sorcerers in the universe.

"They do not understand your powers. But I do. Your power stems from hope and love and truth, whereas theirs stems from decay, indifference, and lies. You will defeat them; I have no doubt. But you must begin your next journey as soon as possible." She paused and readjusted in her seat. "Mordami has found some information you must see. Meet him in the library after your meal; James will be along soon. He has been summoned and would not want to miss something like this." She stood, bowed her head at them, and walked away.

"What is your relationship with my father?" Kala blurted.

Gul stopped walking, turned, and said, "I love him, and I feel he is fond of me. As you know, he will always love your mother. I would never stand between a man and his love, no matter what my own feelings were. After all, I have lost the only man I have loved as much as your parents love one another." A tear slid from her eye, and she walked out the door without showing any other signs of sadness.

Kala regretted asking but didn't regret knowing. She was happy her father had a friend who cared about him, no matter how she cared. Gul would do anything for him, within reason, and for that Kala was grateful. Her father had made a true friend over the years.

The food was ready, and Kala heard her stomach grumble. She had hoped it could be an on-the-go meal, but no such luck. Three courses, beginning with vegetable soup followed by a roast with vegetables and warm bread. For dessert, fruit. Kala could not have been happier for the huge meal. When they ate the meat, they both thanked the pig who had sacrificed itself.

The chef heard them and hugged them, saying, "You truly are who they say you are. Love for the animals, my word! The worlds will be saved."

Kala shivered. It was weird being talked about like this, for someone to… she wouldn't say worship, but adore her like this. Even Daniel had never fawned over her.

When she was full, she stood and said, "Thank you for the meal. Now I'm ready for the library." They had eaten their fruit faster because they couldn't tolerate the kitchen staff hovering. Now it was time to learn what they needed to do next.

The library stood apart from the rest of the manor, up on an enormous wave, solid as the bricked foundation yet appearing to roll throughout its center. She wanted to climb it. "I need to stay motivated," she said to Daniel.

"That was random, but yeah, we all do." Daniel put his hand on her back as they walked up the stairs. Terois Manor, as beautiful and soothing as it was, would haunt their dreams. Kala and Daniel walked fast, eager to learn and then to get out of there.

James stood in the library doorway, watching them as they ascended.

"Daddy, I'm so glad you're here!" Kala picked up her pace but she still couldn't run. The fatigue was enough to make her stop halfway and catch her breath. "I need more time before we leave, I think."

"Yes, you do." Mordami came out, a smile on his face. "Well-deserved time, I would say. What you did was fantastic; my brother studies Carl as we speak, and he is showing massive improvements. One strange thing occurred while you slept—he vomited, and out came a white orb. Based on what we have learned about their race, that may be the power they consumed."

"You mean he vomited out someone's soul?"

"Yes, that is what I mean. Come, I will show you."

Kala followed Mordami and her father over to a table. Dozens of items were labeled with their proposed names and questions written about their purposes. The white orb was rather small, about the size of a marble, and it glowed so brightly it lit the room. The next item, a piece of moonstone, was thought to be part of a larger piece.

One by one, items appeared that would decorate but which Kala could find no other use for. Of course, she was still learning about magic. Growing up isolated from that world did not help her. She closed her eyes and breathed to get back to the moment, then she reached for the moonstone.

"That, I believe, is part of the Roshanra weapon. Legend states the last Roshanra lived four hundred years ago. The weapon was made of moonstone, meant to be unbroken. But when the Roshanra died a horrible death, the weapon split into thousands of pieces. It is said that if a new Roshanra appears, the pieces would begin to travel back towards one another, melding together when they find each other. Once the weapon is complete, they can end their journey. Without the weapon, the world will be overrun by those who call themselves Masters of the world."

Daniel's eyes narrowed. "Why do you call them Masters?"

Mordami appeared to see what Daniel hinted at. "They control the people they consume as much as they controlled the Qurban. In the old text, they were referred to as Masters, but I did not understand until I saw this." Mordami swept his hand across the table. "This," he pointed to an old silver-colored sword, but Kala felt at once that it was not silver at all. The hilt was bare, like the sapphire-bladed dagger she had on her. But she could tell this sword was meant for killing, maiming, destroying, where the dagger was meant to draw blood.

"Oh, shit. I think we need to redo the Qurban antidote."

"Why? What's wrong?"

"When I stabbed Carl, the dagger absorbed some of his blood. I've just worked out the dagger's purpose."

"The blood you got was not of the monster within, it was the man's blood. This man, I do not know if his name was Carl, but I do know that he is all human. Not even magical. His spirit was just strong, so the monster knew he could use him to get to you. He had watched you for most of your life, knowing with certainty it was you the moment you injured yourself and stared at your blood, which flowed off your fingers, instead of crying. He lusted for you. He planned all this to impress his father, who is the king in Tarekana."

"How do you know all this?" Kala's head spun with the information. It appeared the monster was more human than a lot of humans.

"After purging the spirit orb, Carl confessed all."

"Is the threat over?" Kala asked.

James looked at the items, touching each and putting them in a different order. Then he gasped. "No, it's far from over, but we have a reprieve. Take the time you need to regenerate yourself, Kala, eat as much as possible, and don't exercise for a week." He pulled Kala into a hug and said with a whisper, "I'm proud of you, but sorry you had to show me your strength in this way. You will get stronger, and when you do, Daniel and I will both be beside you." He kissed her forehead and turned her towards Daniel.

"You did well," Daniel said again. "I'm proud of you for not giving up like the rest of us did."

"You didn't give up," Kala replied. "We linked and you gave me your power, just like Daddy gave me his. I think I fainted because I put all of me into stopping the terror that was Carl Arresto. I just wanted him gone, but not killed by me. When I thought he was dead, I couldn't handle it. Not because I care about him, no. It was because my values are to show kindness, not hateful and rude gestures. Killing would be hateful, and I won't do it again unless I have to."

"Okay, Kala. Still, you did well. Let's go somewhere relaxing and talk. We haven't talked about anything other than this, and it's time we did."

So they set off to the garden, where they talked and rested and watched water flow between a fountain of swords. It was peaceful, but they knew the peace would not last. Chaos would always return. And they would be ready.

Excerpt from The Crystal of Shamala

Tharlos ripped through the wall that separated dreams from reality. His blood compelled the universe to bend to his will and the cries of the cosmos echoed through his mind. He smiled. Screams were his favorite sound, followed by blood and teardrops dripping onto a metal table.

He stepped into the hallway at Terois Manor. The lab would be to his left and his son would be in a cell nearby. He could smell the mixture of human sweat and rotten meat—that would be Carl. If Tharlos' estimation was correct, he was across the hall from the lab. But his estimations were always correct; he had been a tactician for his whole life, six hundred years and counting.

His boots thumped on the solid water casing and he shook his head. He would have preferred blood over water. What was it with these humans? How were they so weak with the important stuff— torture and murder—yet so strong in others? How had they resisted mutation and compulsion? This wasn't the first time Carl had failed. Maybe he was the weak one.

"Who are you?" A man stood in front of him.

Short and thin—he would never be a good vessel. Tharlos would just have to steal his powers. "Give me your soul," he demanded, snapping his fingers.

The man kneeled and fainted, leaving Tharlos free access to his powers. He opened the man's chest with blackened fingernails, which he extended for the task. Blood poured from the wound; he drank it all. When he was done, he ripped open the man's ribcage and grabbed his heart; it beat weakly in his hand, despite being dry. That was the beauty of blood magic—a victim would live even after they should be dead.

The heart was easy to take, although chewing it took expert skill while inside a vessel. The skill he used today was from a blood specialist from four hundred years ago. The specialist had been a vampire for decades, so he knew his blood. He'd had retractable teeth to go with Tharlos' retractable claws.

The grainy texture excited his senses. He ate with a hunger that only abated when he was done. Once he had licked his fingers clean, he grabbed a keyring from the human's desk. His stomach lurched but he used his powers to control it. He hadn't figured out how to fully control his human body, but he would learn from the spirits he consumed. So far, none had shared their darkest secrets and none had offered information before he asked for it. He wouldn't let his powers degrade, as his father's had. He'd been weak too. That must be where Carl inherited it from.

He opened the cell door. Carl laid in a pool of water, ignoring the bed above him. He was crying! What a weakling.

"Get up! We're leaving."

"What did you do?" Carl whined.

Tharlos' queasiness returned. "I did what you failed to do. I will do the rest on my own as well." He whispered a spell to rip through the fabric of the cosmos. "*Abeta pura, abeta pura, kushaya fabrica anha.*"

The cosmos' cries started anew and Tharlos smiled. Carl followed. He would be punished and rehabilitated… or sacrificed to the God of Torture. There was no other way.

"By the by, you are no longer in line for the throne. That will be the child I rear with the wench; you no longer hold claim to her."

Acknowledgments

Thank you to all who have helped me through this journey!

First, Clem Flanagan, an amazing developmental editor, helped me see what writing skills I have and what I still need to work on. I found her through Reedsy Marketplace and plan to use her services once again.

Second, to Lesley Hart at Author's Pen, who copyedited my book in its final leg. Her corrections brought as much joy as her compliments. She's taught me so much about writing and marketing. I would hire her again in a heartbeat. *www.authorspen.co.uk*

Third, Naomi Reynolds has worked hard on my cover, logo, and helping me set up my website. She's been a great friend over the years. I look forward to working with her more!

And last, but not least, my love, Kenyon. He's been here for me through the years, listening to me ramble on about my story when he has other things to think about. He's here when I need help brainstorming and inspires me every day with his love, encouragement, faith in me, and his music.

SIGN UP FOR THE MONTHLY NEWSLETTER

To receive special offers, giveaways, discounts, bonus content, updates from the author, info on new releases, emotional healing tips, and much more:

https://earnestsbbrown.com